Out of the Darkness

A John Bartley Mystery

By Charles J. Dutton

Originally published in 1922

Out of the Darkness

© 2015 Resurrected Press
www.ResurrectedPress.com

Published by Resurrected Press

This classic book was handcrafted by Resurrected Press. Resurrected Press is dedicated to bringing high quality classic books back to the readers who enjoy them. These are not scanned versions of the originals, but, rather, quality checked and edited books meant to be enjoyed!

Please visit ResurrectedPress.com to view our entire catalogue!

ISBN 13: 978-1-937022-86-0

Printed in the United States of America

Resurrected Press Books in A. E. Fielding's *The Chief Inspector Pointer Mystery* Series

RESURRECTED PRESS CLASSIC MYSTERY CATALOGUE

The Uttermost Farthing: A Savant's Vendetta

Arthur Griffiths
The Passenger From Calais
The Rome Express

Fergus Hume
The Mystery of a Hansom Cab
The Green Mummy
The Silent House
The Secret Passage

Edgar Jepson
The Loudwater Mystery

A. E. W. Mason
At the Villa Rose

A. A. Milne
The Red House Mystery

Baroness Emma Orczy
The Old Man in the Corner

Edgar Allan Poe
The Detective Stories of Edgar Allan Poe

Arthur J. Rees
The Hampstead Mystery
The Shrieking Pit
The Hand In The Dark
The Moon Rock
The Mystery of the Downs

Mary Roberts Rinehart
Sight Unseen and The Confession

Dorothy L. Sayers

Whose Body?

Sir William Magnay
The Hunt Ball Mystery

Mabel and Paul Thorne
The Sheridan Road Mystery

Louis Tracy
The Strange Case of Mortimer Fenley
The Albert Gate Mystery
The Bartlett Mystery
The Postmaster's Daughter
The House of Peril
The Sandling Case: What Would You Have Done?

Charles Edmonds Walk
The Paternoster Ruby

John R. Watson
The Mystery of the Downs
The Hampstead Mystery

Edgar Wallace
The Daffodil Mystery
The Crimson Circle

Carolyn Wells
Vicky Van
The Man Who Fell Through the Earth
In the Onyx Lobby
Raspberry Jam
The Clue
The Room with the Tassels
The Vanishing of Betty Varian
The Mystery Girl
The White Alley
The Curved Blades

FOREWORD

The 1920's and 1930's are one of the most interesting periods in the history of detective fiction. On the one hand, it was the "Golden Age" of British mysteries with such authors as Agatha Christie, Dorothy L. Sayers, Anthony Berkeley along with many others producing a body of work that was both literate and genteel. The emphasis was on the puzzle element of the crime, with authors vying with each other to create the most ingenious methods of murder. On the other side of the Atlantic, authors such as Carroll John Daly, Dashiell Hammett, and Raymond Chandler were inventing a far different type of detective fiction. This hard-boiled school focused on the seamier aspects of society where the success of the detective depended more on his abilities with fist and gun than cleverness.

Yet not all authors of mysteries can be so easily classified as belonging to one camp or the other. This was particularly true in America where many authors adopted aspects of both styles in their works. Charles J. Dutton was one of these authors.

On the surface, Dutton would seem an unlikely author of mysteries. University educated, he studied both the law and theology. He worked for a period of time as a journalist before finally taking up a post as minister in a church in Iowa. While a minister, he was a frequent contributor to of uplifting articles to *The Reader's Digest*. Yet, in the 20's and early 30's he authored sixteen mystery novels as well as numerous short stories. His works have none of the raw violence that characterize the hard-boiled school, but, written for the most part during the era of Prohibition, there is a dark undercurrent of crime and lawlessness below the "respectable" society on which the books are centered.

His early works feature John Bartley, who, as a detective, is in some ways almost a throwback to the Edwardian examples of the profession. A man of means, education, and breeding, he solves the crimes of the wealthy and powerful by force of intellect. But even Bartley finds himself involved with subjects that were taboo for many authors of the time, such as racism and religious fundamentalism. This is particularly true in the novel *The Crooked Cross*.

His second series of mysteries focus on Harley Manners, a professor of abnormal and criminal psychology. Rather than the "How", Professor Manners is much more concerned with the "Why" a crime was committed. His success as an investigator owes as much to his understanding of the human mind, particularly its dark side, as to physical clues. The villains in the six books of the series are motivated as much by a psychological pathology as by greed or lust. As if to accentuate this dual nature of good and evil, his two best friends are Rogan the chief of police and Zuko, a prominent underworld figure.

Out of the Darkness, the second book in the series of nine featuring John Bartley, is actually a two part mystery. The first case involves two men convicted of burglary in a case that bears a remarkable resemblance to a nineteenth century British case in which two men were wrongly convicted through manufactured evidence. The second case involves the murder of the man whose house it was where the modern burglary took place. The central question of the book is whether the two crimes are related or whether it is just a coincidence.

There are several subthemes that run through *Out of the Darkness*. The first of these has to do with the consumption of illegal alcohol. The book, as were all except the last of Dutton's mysteries, was written during Prohibition. Yet his characters, from the police chief on down, regularly consume imported whisky, brandy and wine. The book highlights one of the paradoxes of the Prohibition Era which is that America's attitude towards alcohol became more positive and that people drank more after Prohibition was instituted than before the passage of the Volstead Act. That drinking should play such a large role in his books is curious considering that Dutton later went on to become a Unitarian minister and author of uplifting articles for *The Reader's Digest*.

The second subtheme has to do with the after effects of the First World War, which had only been over for a few years when the book was written. In a number of the descriptions of characters reference is made to their wearing a pin on their lapel indicating service in France. Bartley, himself, did not serve in the war because he had been engaged by the Secret Service for counter-espionage work. A point is made of the fact that Dr. King, the coroner, suffers from shell-shock, later to become known as battle-fatigue during World War II, and now referred to as Post Traumatic Stress Disorder or P.T.S.D. Shell-shock features prominently in many mysteries of the 1920's such as *The Shrieking Pit* showing how badly the war had scarred the public psyche.

Another result of the war's aftermath was the rise of Spiritualism, as many people attempted to contact the victims of that conflict. As remarked on in the book, the interest in Spiritualism has seen a revival after every major conflict. This was certainly true during the 1920's where many otherwise rational people held their skepticism in abeyance on the subject. Séances and mediums were staples of the mysteries of the period, often serving to reveal a murderer, and Dutton was to use them as a device for that purpose on more than one occasion.

While somewhat forgotten as a mystery writer today, Charles J. Dutton was an author who could look into the darker side of human nature. For this reason his novels should still be of interest to the modern reader. It is therefore, with pleasure that Resurrected Press introduces this new edition of *Out of the Darkness*.

About the Author

Charles J. Dutton (1888-1964) was an American writer of mysteries. He was educated at Brown University and later studied at Albany Law School and the Defiance Theological Seminary. After graduation he worked for a while as a newspaper columnist. He wrote numerous works of fiction that were published in magazines both in the U.S. and Great Britain. In the early 1930's he moved to Des Moines, Iowa where he assumed the post of minister for the First Unitarian Church. He wrote some fifteen mystery novels. Appearing in nine of these was the private detective John Bartley. Bartley was followed by Professor Harley Manners, a criminal psychologist who was featured in six novels. The two characters overlap in the book *Streaked With Crimson*. One of the things that set Dutton apart from other mystery writers of the period was his interest in the psychology of the criminal mind. He was also fascinated by old books and ancient history, subjects which play parts in a number of his novels.

Greg Fowlkes
Editor-In-Chief
Resurrected Press
www.ResurrectedPress.

TABLE OF CONTENTS

I. In Which An Old Crime Again Comes To Light

THAT Friday afternoon, as I came up the steps of John Bartley's house in Gramercy Square, the sun was shining for the first time in seven days. The children who had been kept in the house for a week by the rain were playing in the street and laughing loudly, in sheer glee at being out again. For a moment or two I watched them, waving my hand to several little girls racing by. Then, unlocking the door, I entered the hall and went up the stairs to my room.

This week of rain in the middle of June had spoiled Bartley's long planned fishing trip, and had kept us in the city. It was a trip he had been looking forward to for a long time, since in the past few years there had been few opportunities for such things. In fact, since 1917 Bartley had passed very few nights in his own house. About a year before we went into the war, those who followed criminal mysteries noticed that Bartley's name was no longer connected with the solution of crime. Perhaps they wondered a little at this. When the full story of the work of the Secret Service in the war is told, recognition will be given to the part he played in bringing it to a victorious conclusion. Until then, all I can say is that when he returned to New York, in the spring of 1920, his work for the government had ended.

The first thing that he did upon his arrival was to clear up a pile of mail that ran back for several years; his next was to plan several weeks' fishing in the lakes of northern Maine. On the very day that we were to start it had commenced to rain, and never ceased for seven days.

Telegrams told us that in Maine it was raining, too. In sheer disgust Bartley buried himself in his library and went to work on his long neglected book, "*The Galante Literature of the 18th Century.*"

As I glanced out of the window of my room that Friday afternoon, I saw that the rain was at last over. I was wondering whether Bartley would go to Maine after all, when there came a rap on my door. Opening it, I found Ranee, Hartley's old colored man, who said with a grin, "Mr. John says, Mr. Pelt, that you are to come down into the library, for that man Rogers is coming."

As I followed him down the stairs, I wondered what it was that was bringing Rogers, chief of the Central Office, to the house at this time of the afternoon. Although Rogers and Bartley were the best of friends, and the chief had been forced more than once to ask the aid of Bartley in his cases, he usually made his visits in the evening, after the day's work was over. A call at four in the afternoon seemed to promise that something unusual had happened, something of such importance that it could not wait. Could he secure Bartley's aid? I knew that Bartley had not intended to take up any more cases until he had had a long rest. Still, if Rogers had the problem of some unusual crime to lay before us, he might change his plans.

He was in his library, that room which to me was the most wonderful room in the city. When he had made over the house and moved into it, he said that, at last, he had the kind of a library that he had always wanted. All the partitions on the first floor had been torn away and a great room left, extending almost the entire length of the house. In the center of the wall across from the door was a great fireplace, almost high enough for a man to stand in, its two sides flanked by great benches that ran into the stone work. On all sides, to a height of six feet, were book cases containing the wonderful library, to which he was continually adding.

One wall housed hundreds of rare "Memoires," the intimate living documents of the highly colored life of France and Italy, from the sixteenth century onward. But the most interesting thing in the room, perhaps, was his collection of the records of criminal trials which filled the cases on the opposite side. Here were hundreds of pamphlets, transcripts of old trials, confessions of criminals, and details of notable crimes from all countries. I have never been able to estimate how many there were, for it was a collection unrivaled in the country and the list ran well into the thousands. Above the book cases the walls were covered with scores of valuable etchings and prints, most of them originals. Bartley used to say that one good print was worth a hundred poor paintings; and here he had signed etchings of Rops, of Whistler, of Beardsley, and of Rowlandson, the gay French prints of Boucher, Fragonard, Deveuna and Baudoin. Anyone looking at the room would have known that it belonged to a bookish man, but few would have ever dreamed that it also was the library of a criminal investigator.

Bartley was at his great desk when I entered. He gave me a smile, then went on examining the books which covered its top. That morning he had received a great box from his French dealer, and he was busy with its contents. As he did not speak, I dropped into the great arm chair by his side.

As I looked at him I wondered, as I had done so many times before, that he should be the great criminal investigator that he was. It was the last thing anyone would expect him to be. His breeding, his family, and above all his literary tastes, were not such as one would expect to find in a man who makes the running down of criminals his life work. His fine face with its clear cut features, telling of a long line of New England ancestors, might have been a bishop's, one that loved dogs and children, and who had a heart bigger than his creed. The fact that his hair had begun to be tinged with gray gave an added distinction to his appearance. His long fingers were turning the pages of the book he held with the loving touch that all real booklovers have when handling rare editions. I picked up one of the six thin, narrow books in heavy gray paper covers that lay before him, and glanced at the title, "*The Ragionamenti of the Divine Aretino.*" I was about to open it when the doorbell rang.

Bartley glanced up at the sound and said, "That must be Rogers."

The next moment Ranee, bowing as he always did in announcing anyone, ushered Rogers into the room. Rogers had been at the head of the Central Office for about five years. In that time he had built up for himself the finest reputation that any city detective had ever had. He was not a brilliant man, nor, for that matter, an educated one, but his rare common sense and his absolute honesty had won for him the respect of the people of the city. He was a heavy man, with a very red face filled with good humor, and the slow movements that so many police officers have.

He took a chair, and after saying "Hello, John" to Bartley and a word to me, he took a cigar from the box that Bartley pushed over to him and, leaning across the table, picked up one of the volumes. The book fell open at a picture; he started as he looked at it, then handed it to me with a sly wink.

"That's a fine sort of a book to show an honest and moral police officer. If I found a bookseller on the Avenue with one, I would have him pinched."

Bartley swung around in his chair, saw which book it was, and laughed.

"Well, Rogers," he said, "the man that wrote that book died a good many hundred years ago. He was the greatest adventurer of his day, the first real blackmailer, a man that made his living by his wits. Also, he happened to be a poet and dramatist, as well as a rogue."

Rogers took his cigar from his mouth and responded with a grin, "What we call today a crook."

I could see that there was something on the chief's mind, but just what it was we were not to learn for some time. He talked, first about the rain, then about the baseball team, in fact of everything but the purpose that had brought him. That was his way, as we both knew. It was not until he had lighted a second cigar and had been silent several moments that he turned to Bartley and said:

"John, I have a case for you."

Bartley threw me a quick glance, then answered, "But you know, Rogers, I don't care to take up any more cases until I have been away fishing and had a good rest."

The chief nodded, but added, "Well, this won't be much of a case. It's not my affair, anyway. I happened to see the Governor the other day, and he asked me to get you to look into the matter and make him a report."

I glanced at Bartley. The Governor of the State did not, as a rule, interest himself in criminal matters. If this was a case that he wished Bartley to investigate, then it must be something very unusual, indeed. By the little gleam of interest in his eyes, I could see that he agreed with me.

"What is the case?" he asked.

"Well," answered Rogers after a short pause, "I don't suppose you know anything about it; though you may have seen it mentioned in the papers since you returned. It all started a year ago. It was a robbery."

Bartley gave a little exclamation of disgust. "You know that robbery cases are out of my line. There is never anything of interest in them. Besides, a robbery that took place a year ago must be all settled by this time."

Rogers took his cigar from his lips, tried to blow a smoke ring, failed, and simply said, "Well, the two chaps that they say committed this robbery are now in jail with a seven years' stretch over them."

This mystified me, and I could see that even Bartley was puzzled. A crime for which two men were already serving a seven years' sentence did not seem to promise much of a case, and Bartley said as much.

Rogers was now willing to tell all that he knew; and placing his cigar in the tray, he leaned back in his chair, and began:

"You know, John, after all, I don't know such a devil of a lot about this thing myself. I got mixed up in it by accident. I happened to see the Governor on another matter; and when I had finished my business, he told me he had received a good many letters asking him to pardon the men that were in jail for the Circle Lake robbery. Many of these letters were from lawyers, in which they said that, after they had read the evidence, they doubted if the men were guilty. Also, one of these reform societies has got mixed up in the thing. The Governor had read the evidence brought out at the trial, and he believed himself that the men might not be guilty of the robbery. Then he asked me if you were in the city; and, when I said 'Yes,' he suggested that I ask you to look into the affair. If you, after having investigated the matter, think the men are innocent, then he will pardon them. He said, also, that there was some sort of a fund from which he could pay your fee."

Bartley gave me a curious look, then turned to Rogers. "That part's all right, Rogers. Only I haven't the faintest idea what you are talking about. Of course, I know where Circle Lake is. It's near Saratoga. A friend of mine has a summer place there. But beyond that, I have no idea what you are driving at. Why not start at the beginning and tell me what this crime was?"

With a grin the chief started at the beginning of the story.

"Of course, you know who Robert Slyke is?"

Bartley nodded; but, seeing that I did not recognize the name, he turned to me.

"Pelt, don't you remember the Wall Street broker who announced at a Billy Sunday meeting that he had been converted, and that he was going to give back to his clients the money they had lost in his office?"

Both Bartley and Rogers laughed, and the latter commented, "He never gave it back."

"No," said Bartley, "he never did. That conversion did not stick. Slyke is a strange sort of a chap. His friends are few and there have been wild rumors as to where he got his money. He has dabbled a bit in spiritualism, and has been fooled by several mediums."

Rogers nodded in agreement. "That's the chap. He has a place at Circle Lake. He has lived there for the last two years all the year round. No one knows exactly why he left the city, but it is said that he has lost a lot of money in stocks."

He paused, then continued, "It was Slyke who had the robbery. Early one morning, about a year ago, his step daughter came to his room and said there were burglars downstairs. He jumped from his bed, and, without any weapon, rushed down the stairs, while the girl stayed on the top step. From then on, it becomes mixed up."

"Mixed up?" asked Bartley.

"Yes. Just what took place and how many men were in the room at the time, was a point of dispute at the trial. The girl says she is sure—that is, almost sure—there were two men in the room. On the other hand, Slyke says there was only one; though, he added, there might have been a second man whom he did not see. There was a bit of a struggle, and the men jumped out of an open window and got away."

Bartley, who had listened carefully, asked, "They did not get anything?"

"No, not a thing. Slyke swore up and down at the trial that there was nothing in the house that they could have been after, that he never kept any money there. The safe in the room was unopened."

"Are these men," asked Bartley, "the ones that are serving the seven years' sentence?"

Rogers paused long enough to light another cigar, and throw back his head to watch the smoke curl to the ceiling before he replied, "That's the big question."

He was silent for a moment, then continued:

"After the burglars got out of the window, Slyke called up the city police and also the state police. When the city police arrived at the house they made no arrests. But early that same morning the state police picked up two men about six miles away on the other side of Saratoga. They were both well known characters who had been in trouble before. They were found sneaking through the fields, trying to get home without being seen. One of the men had a slight bruise on his head. Slyke claimed that in the struggle he hit one of the robbers with a cane. Both men refused to say where they had been during the night. The strange thing about it was that they were taken to their own homes before being locked up. When they were searched, the police found nothing on them whatever."

Bartley was interested. He took up his pipe, lighted it, and leaning back in his chair, listened attentively as Rogers continued.

"When it came time for the men to be identified, there was a bit of a conflict. The step-daughter was pretty sure that there had been two men, while Slyke insisted that he had only seen one. In fact, he did not seem to be very eager to push the case—even requested the police to drop it since he had lost nothing.

Bartley asked in surprise, "Then why, under heaven, did they keep on with it?"

Rogers shook his head. 'I don't know, John. It has been suggested that the city police did not want to drop it. There is a good deal of jealousy between the local police of the small towns and the state body; and there had been trouble recently with the particular state police who made the arrests. Anyway, they held the men; and a few days later announced that they had found a piece of paper torn from a newspaper in the room where Slyke had discovered them. Several days later they announced that they had found a newspaper with a torn corner in Horn's pocket, into which the piece that they had found at Slyke's house fitted."

Bartley asked with a weary air, "Did they later find a piece "of cloth torn from the coat or trousers of one of the men? Find it, perhaps, on a bush near the window the men had jumped out of?"

Rogers gave his friend a startled look.

"I thought you had never heard of the case? They did find such a piece of cloth."

Bartley half laughed. "I never heard a word of it until you told me. I had an idea that a piece of cloth would be found that had been torn from the clothing of one of them. A piece that would fit, say, the torn trousers of one of them."

Rogers threw me a look, as if to ask how Bartley could have guessed, then remarked, "I don't see how you hit it off, John; but that's the very thing that did happen. All this did not come out until the trial. When it was introduced, it made a stir. Both men denied up and down that they had ever been in the house, or even near it. Horn said that he never had had a newspaper in his pocket. They both claimed, in fact, that the whole thing was a frame up."

He paused to relight his cigar before continuing:

"The man to whom the trousers belonged asserted that they had been taken from him the week after he had been put in jail, and that there was no tear in them when he gave them up. A tailor at the trial testified that the cloth was so strong that it could not have been torn away by catching on anything, and that it looked to him as if the piece had been cut out with a knife."

Bartley threw back his head and laughed. Why he should be amused I could not imagine. He asked, "How about the footprints?"

Bartley's manner seemed to puzzle Rogers. He admitted, however, that there were footprints, though he did not know where they had been found, nor when. "No one heard of most of the evidence until the trial," he added.

Once more Bartley laughed, and this time Rogers was thoroughly displeased. "I don't see the joke."

"There is no joke, Rogers. Tell me who found all this evidence? Was it the police?"

"I am not sure. I think it was the head of the local police. It was a day or so after the crime that most of it was discovered."

I broke in to say, "I presume the men claimed the police faked the evidence?"

Rogers nodded. "That's just what they did claim. In fact, their whole defence was on that line. They were said to have been night fishing on a game preserve near the lake. They denied that they had ever been within five miles of Slyke's house. A good deal was made of the fact that the incriminating evidence was not found until some hours after the crime—even days in fact. I admit that it looks a bit fishy. Still, you never heard of the police faking evidence to the extent they claim this was done."

We both laughed, and our laughter made the red face of the chief turn a shade darker. We had in mind the charges that one of the newspapers was making at the time against his own detectives, that they had planted guns on some men they wished to hold. But even at that, he was right. The police do not fake evidence to the extent that this story of his seemed to hint. Bartley's next remark showed that he felt as I did.

"You are right, Rogers, though the whole thing does look queer. First, Slyke's not being able to recognize the men, then his desire not to have them brought to trial, and lastly the discovery of most of the evidence so much later. I take it the conviction made a stir."

Rogers shook his head. "It did not at the time; it's doing it now. The papers thought the men's denial was the usual thing. But later the lawyers got interested, then a reform society, and now they are all getting after the Governor. He thinks there might have been a miscarriage of justice and wants you to look into the thing. He wants you to do it at once!'

With a shrewd look, Bartley asked, "Then there is something new?"

"Well," answered Rogers, "that depends. The other night there was another attempt to break into Slyke's house. They say there have been several since these men went to jail."

Bartley said but one word, but it was expressive enough. We sat in silence until Rogers pulled out his watch, glanced at it, and rose to his feet. "Time I ran along. That's the way it stands. The Governor wishes you to look into it, and says he will consider it as a personal favor if you will do so."

Bartley also rose, and placing his hand on his friend's shoulder, said, "I will deal with the case at once, but in my own way. Tell him he won't hear from me until I have found out whether those two men ought to be in prison or not."

Rogers nodded, and after a second glance at his watch hurried out. After his departure, Bartley picked up the little book he had been studying, fingered it for a moment, then with a little sigh placed it back on the desk. He was half regretting, I knew, that he had given his word to Rogers to look into the matter. I wondered why he had taken up a burglary case, one moreover, that had been committed a year ago. As a rule, the only cases that interested him were the unusual ones that had a mystery in them that it was almost impossible to solve. This type of crime was usually a murder. Yet here he was interested in a simple burglary case! Our fishing trip, too, was evidently off. I could not understand the situation at all.

As if reading my mind, Bartley said, "Pelt, over in the book case, in the section of the trials, you will find a small brown book. It's somewhere in the third section, under the letter E. The title is, I think, *'The Edlingham Burglary'*."

Wondering a little why he should want it, I went over to the portion of the book case he had indicated. There seemed to be a good many that started with "E." Most of them were little thin pamphlets, printed on the poorest of paper. In a moment I had found the volume that he wanted—a thin book, covered with brown cloth, and on the title page

The Famous Edlingham Burglary
or
The Innocent Persecuted
1879

I handed Bartley the book, and without a word he opened it and quickly ran through the pages. In a few minutes he threw it over to me, saying with a smile, "I know, Pelt, you are wondering why we should spend our time on a simple burglary case; but this may turn out to be a rather curious one. You know we say that there are no two crimes alike in every detail. Yet when Rogers told me the story of that Circle Lake affair, I recognized at once that it resembled a very famous case that took place in England in 1879."

In surprise I remarked, "You did?"

He waited to fill and light his pipe before continuing:

"Yes, that's why I am interested in it. It's almost the same in every detail as the story you will find in that pamphlet you hold in your hand. The English case, known in criminal history as *'The Edlingham Burglary,'* is famous because two innocent men were in prison for six years for a crime they did not commit. The evidence against them, the manner in which it was discovered, is almost, if not the very same as that in this affair at Circle Lake of which Rogers tells us."

Impressed, I could only exclaim, "That's queer!"

Bartley nodded. "It's more than queer. The Edlingham case goes down in the history of crime as one of the worst miscarriages of justice of which we know. There is no doubt that the police faked the evidence against the men. They spent six years in prison for a crime they knew nothing about. In that case, too, the two men were found early in the morning in the house of a local vicar. Just as Slyke and his step daughter found someone in their house, so the vicar and his daughter discovered two men in their living room. Later the men were arrested on the outskirts of the little English village; and, as in the story that Rogers told us, a piece of paper was found in the room at the vicarage that fitted into the torn corner of a newspaper which was discovered some days later in the house of one of the men. Footprints were also found under the window, and a little piece of cloth on a rose bush. This in turn fitted into a torn place in a pair of trousers belonging to one of the men."

I uttered an exclamation of wonder, and Bartley grinned. "Now the strange thing here, too, is that none of this evidence was discovered at first. The men declared at the trial that they were innocent, and it was not until years afterward that it was learned that the police had faked the evidence. It is the most famous case of its kind in the history of English crime. It's odd how the evidence in this Circle Lake robbery parallels it so closely. It looks a little as if someone had read of the English crime, and tried to repeat the evidence in this one."

The thought that two men might be in jail for a crime which they had never committed, might even know nothing of, went against the grain. I asked, "And then these men may be innocent?"

"Well," replied Bartley, thoughtfully, "maybe. The fact that there have been other attempts to break into Slyke's house points that way. To a student of criminal literature, the finding of an old crime re staged is rather interesting. That is why I said I would look into it."

I now thoroughly understood Bartley's willingness to forego his fishing trip. There was more in this burglary than appeared on the surface.

"Go into the office, will you, Pelt, and see what we
have there on Slyke."

Bartley had a large office opening from his library,
where his secretary worked and where he received his
clients. It was lined with tall, green filing cabinets,
containing the reports of his cases and his wonderful card
index. This index contained information about almost
every important person in the country, information that
gave at a glance a keen insight into the character of the
man whose name was on the card. It took me but a
second to find the card that contained Slyke's name.
When I returned to the library, Bartley asked me to read
it aloud. It contained the following:

"Slyke, Robert, broker. Born Kittery, Maine. Educated
in Public School. In business in New Hampshire, 1879
to 1886, buying and trading cattle. Came to New
York, 1886, became a broker. Made and lost several
fortunes. Said to have been converted by Billy Sunday
in 1913; no evidence of it. Rather eccentric, dabbled a
bit in spiritualism and has been duped by several
mediums. Quick tempered, with few friends. There is
a question of his business honesty. Wife died 1914.
One son and a step daughter. Summer home, Circle
Lake, N. Y. City home, Garden City. Was worth about
$500,000, but rumored to have lost a good part of this
in recent years."

Bartley listened while I read this short and
commonplace history.

When I had finished, he said simply, "Nothing much
there. I have never heard, in fact, anything of importance
about him. On the Street he played a lone hand, had few
friends, and as few enemies. It's curious he is mixed up in
an affair of this kind. I wonder what was in his house
that the burglars wanted."

I asked the question that had been in my mind for some time. "Why was he unable to identify the men when his daughter said she could?"

Bartley smiled at my question. "You are getting wiser every day, Pelt. It is curious that Slyke professed to be unable to identify the men when the girl, who was on the steps behind him and even further away from the men than he was, could do so. It may be he was right and she wrong. It may even be that he did recognize them and did not want to say who they were. If that is so, then the whole affair is more mysterious than ever."

He rose to his feet and glanced at his watch. "Tomorrow, or Sunday, we will run up to the lake. We had better drive up in my car. It will take only seven hours. I will telegraph to Currie, my old Harvard roommate, that we are coming. He has been after me for several years to come for a visit."

He walked the length of the room, and paused a moment to study attentively a Rops highly colored etching, much as if he had never seen it before. Then he turned back to the desk and said, "You had better read over that pamphlet of the Edlingham case now. The two cases are curiously similar."

As he left the room, he added with a regretful little laugh, "There goes our fishing; it's always the way."

An hour later when he returned I was still curled up in a big chair by the fireplace. I had spent the time reading the story of the old English crime. The two cases were, as Bartley had said, very much alike. Making due allowance for time and place, I wondered that two cases, happening so many years apart, could so resemble each other in every detail. I agreed with Bartley that, if we took the ground that someone at Circle Lake had faked the evidence, then whoever he was he had read the report of this other crime and used it as a guide. I laid the book aside and glanced up at him.

From the little smile on his face and the cheery tone in his voice as he entered, no one would have supposed that once again he was beginning a criminal investigation.

"Well, Pelt, if you have read it, we have just time to run over to Clark's for dinner and get to the theater before the curtain goes up on the first act of Drinkwater's '*Lincoln*.' It's the third time we have seen it, but it's worth seeing again."

He turned and went out into the hall. Before I could rise and follow him, I heard his voice urging, "Hurry, Pelt, it's late now."

II. In Which We Visit Mr. Slyke, But Do Not Receive A Very Warm Reception

IT was not until early Sunday morning that we were able to leave the city. After the days of rain, the ride along the banks of the Hudson was very beautiful. The sun was out, bright and warm, and there was no dust. We rode for miles with well kept estates, their green lawns brightened with patches of flowers on one side, and on the other, its surface glimmering in the sun, the river, dotted here and there with boats.

Though Bartley is, as a rule, more or less silent, yet, when he is driving a car, he talks all the time. His knowledge of literature and his criticisms of life and history made the time pass quickly. Bartley is one of those people that really live. Nothing that men and women have ever been interested in fails to stir his interest. That is, nothing but music. Literature is a hobby, art he knows a great deal about—he is more or less an authority on prints—but good music arouses an intense hatred. He made so many interesting comments on the local history of the towns through which we drove that almost before I knew it we were in Albany.

We had luncheon in one of the large hotels to the accompaniment of an orchestra booming the popular music of the moment. Bartley was so thoroughly uncomfortable that he refused to speak. It was not until we were waiting for the waiter to return with our change and he had lighted a cigar that he became more amiable. He bowed to some people he knew, then leaned toward me and spoke softly so that those at the next table would not hear.

"Pelt, we cannot say just what we will find up at the lake. I have thought the affair over carefully, and the more I think of it the more puzzled I am. If Rogers told us all the facts, then there are two well defined conclusions to be drawn. The first is that those two men are innocent. The second is that Slyke knew who it was that broke into his house, but had strong reasons for claiming he could not recognize them. If his daughter could swear to the identity of the men that were arrested, he should also have been able to recognize them. But he says he did not, and, we are told, he wanted the case dropped."

He paused as the waiter appeared with our change, and we went back to our car.

Saratoga was only a forty five mile drive from Albany. Circle Lake was several miles nearer. We ran slowly up State Street, past that queer mass of architecture we call the Capitol, and then by the beautiful "Education Building," and so out into the country.

I knew very little about Circle Lake except that it was a small lake outside of Saratoga where there were a number of large summer estates. Bob Currie, who had roomed with Bartley at Harvard, had a place there where he passed the greater part of the year. Currie was one of the few men that had won a warm place in Bartley's heart. Two men more unlike it would have been hard to find. Bartley was a man of culture and a lover of books, while Currie never read a book if he could help it. He was a shrewd broker who made his money in Wall Street and spent it on his farm. It was far different from the kind of farm the average rich man owns. Currie's actually paid, a feat that pleased him far more than the thousands of dollars that his brokerage firm made each year. A better hearted or more lovable man never lived.

About an hour and a half out of Albany, Bartley said suddenly, pointing to a small sheet of water in the distance, "That's Circle Lake."

We were on the top of a large hill at the moment, and, though the lake was several miles away, it looked even smaller than I had expected. It was not more than a mile across, and was a complete circle except where a small bay broke its circumference. It was nearly surrounded by trees and, as our car dropped down the steep descent, it sank out of sight among them.

At the foot of the hill, the road ran beside the lake for a little way, then ascended another hill. Just before this ascent began, Bartley left the main road and followed one that ran for nearly a mile between leafy trees. Every once in a while I caught glimpses of white houses, set far back from the highway and almost hidden among them. At length Bartley turned his car down a long driveway that wound its crooked way in and out through a grove of great trees. When I had begun to wonder if we should ever escape from them, we came out upon a green lawn that stretched for several acres, having in its midst a large rambling house, painted the whitest white I have ever seen. It was a cheery looking house, one made to live in, with a great piazza stretching across the front, and gay-covered chairs that gave to it a tropical atmosphere. Even as I was thinking how much I liked it, a man came running down the steps, three at a time, whooping like a wild Indian and waving his arms at us.

Truth compels me to say that Currie was, to put it mildly, stout, nor could anyone call him good looking. His big red face, now almost purple from exercise, was a kindly, tolerant one, filled with humor; his blue eyes warm with kindness. Down the steps he came and across the lawn, yelling all the time:

"John Bartley, you old sleuth, don't you dare drive on my new lawn!"

With a laugh, Bartley made a wide circle across the grass before he stopped. Currie was beside us and on the step of the car in a second, one arm thrown around Bartley's shoulder and his red face beaming; but all he said was, "Well, well, John!"

Bartley's answer was just as short and had the same deep friendliness. Then Currie turned and greeted me. A second later, a servant came to take charge of our things, and we followed Currie to the house.

He continued delightedly, as we mounted the steps to the piazza, "So you are actually going to make me a visit, John. It's about time you did. I can show you the finest farm you ever laid your eyes on. One that gives the lie to the old yarn that a business man can't run a farm profitably. Cows, why, I have some of the finest cows you ever saw. And—"

Bartley laughed, and, winking at me, interrupted solemnly, "Bob, I am going to make you a visit, but only on one condition."

Currie stopped with a puzzled look. "One condition? What is it?"

Bartley, his face serious but his eyes dancing, replied, "Yes, on one condition. It is that you do not kill me by talking about your farm. I am willing to agree that as a farmer you are a wizard. In fact, after what happened to that stock I bought on your advice, I am even willing to admit you may be a better farmer than a broker. I am willing to agree without even looking at them, that you have the best cows in the state. Yes, pigs even. But I don't give a damn for all the cows and pigs that ever lived. I came up here to see you, not the farm." With this he reached over and slapped his friend on the back; and Currie grinned back at him in the perfect understanding of close friendship.

"All right, John," he said. "I won't talk any more about the farm, if that will keep you here longer. But, honestly, I have the finest—" And at that we all laughed.

We entered the house by one of the largest living rooms that I have ever seen. It stretched almost the entire length of the building and had two fireplaces, both of which were large enough for a man to stand upright in. Currie led us up a flight of stairs to the second story where, pushing open a door, he showed us into our suite of rooms. Without giving us time to get our bearings, he motioned for us to come to the window and see his view. It was well worth seeing. Far to the north were the mountains, dark blue against the lighter blue of the sky.

Nearer, looking so close that it seemed as if we could almost drop a stone into it, lay Saratoga, its white church steeples rising far above the green tree tops. By turning a little we caught a glimpse of Saratoga Lake, its surface, under the June sun, calm and still; and at our feet, stretching away to a patch of woods, the cool green fields of Currie's farm.

Five minutes later, at Currie's suggestion, the three of us were sitting on the stone edge of his swimming pool. It was forty feet long and open to sun and air. On its granite edge were wicker chairs, shaded from the sight of the passers by by a trellis covered with early roses. For thirty minutes we swam and dived, Currie yelling most of the time like a boy. Then we climbed out and dried ourselves in the warm sun. As Currie pressed a bell, he asked with a grin if we had any objection to breaking the Eighteenth Amendment.

It was not until we had finished our third mint julep and Bartley had lighted a cigarette that he told his friend what had brought us to Circle Lake.

Currie said nothing until he had finished, and then, rubbing his chin slowly with his hand, replied, "Do you know, John, there are a good many people around here that doubt if those two men had anything to do with the robbery. There was nothing stolen, so Slyke said. He said also that there was nothing in the house that anyone would want to steal. After the trial folks began to talk, and since those other attempts to break into his place— well, they have talked more!"

"What are they saying?" asked Bartley.

"I don't know such a devil of a lot about it myself," replied Currie, "I was away at the time of the burglary and of the trial. But I do know that some people doubt if there ever was a burglary. Others say the state police and the local cops got mixed up in a row and framed the men. Still others that Slyke knew who the men were, but had strong reasons for not wanting to identify them. What his reasons could be, God alone knows! Never cottoned much to Slyke anyway. He is a crabbed sort of chap, a bit conceited, one who is always right and the rest of us, of course, always wrong. But if you want to see him, and are not too tired, we can go over there now. I have to see him myself about a strip of land I just bought from him. His estate joins mine, you know."

Bartley expressed himself as far from tired and very willing to go to see Slyke at once. We dressed quickly and soon joined Currie in the living room. As we went out onto the lawn, he said:

"I am sorry my wife is away, but she will be back tomorrow. I asked Doctor King to come over tonight and dine with us. He is the doctor here, was in the army during the war, and is a bookworm like you, John. He can probably tell you more about the robbery than I can, for he was called in by Slyke the night it happened."

We left the house by a little path that followed a small brook through a large field until it came to some woods. The air was sweet with the smell of pines, birds sang, and a flower gleamed here and there. After a ten minutes' walk we came suddenly upon a house. The woods came within a few yards of its rear, but as we walked around to the front we saw that it faced on a large park containing some ten acres of land. The lawn, closely cropped, ended in a sunken garden in which a fountain played. Under the dancing sunlight, as it was blown to and fro by the slight breeze, its spray turned all of the colors of the rainbow.

The house itself was a massive stone building, half covered with ivy. A large veranda ran across the front, forming at one end a glass enclosed sun parlor. What appealed to me most was the huge stone tower that rose from the center of the building to a height of some thirty feet. It was one of the few towers that I have seen in this country, that looked as if it were a part of the house itself and not an addition put on as an afterthought. The house, with its well kept lawn, stretching to the woods in the distance, made a beautiful picture.

Though we had not paused long to admire the scene, we did not have time to ascend the steps and ring the bell before the butler opened the door. Currie gave his name and we were ushered into a great room which, from its furnishings, might have been called a library if there had been any books in it. At the far end was a flight of stairs leading to the second story, that separated at a landing half way up into two narrower flights running at right angles to each other.

When the butler had left us, Bartley said to Currie, "I presume that this is the room where they found the burglars?"

Currie nodded, and I turned to look about. It had two large windows opening on the side of the house where there was no veranda, and nearby a small safe, half hidden in the wall. This, I judged, must have been what the burglars were seeking. I tried to picture to myself what had taken place on the night of the burglary. There could not have been much light; and I wondered how Slyke's step-daughter, standing on the stairs at the far end of the room, could have seen well enough to recognize the men, when Slyke, who was close by, could not do so.

I had little time for my conjectures, for at that moment Slyke entered the room. After greeting Currie, he was introduced to us. He gave me a clammy, moist hand, the kind of a hand I hate to touch. I had expected that when Bartley's name was mentioned he would show some surprise, but the name evidently meant nothing to him; or if it did, he did not associate the man before him with the well known criminal investigator.

While Currie was talking with him about the strip of land that he had bought, I examined him closely.

He was a small, decidedly nervous man, weighing about a hundred and thirty pounds, with low forehead, shifty eyes, and flabby lips that drooped. His face twitched again and again and his hands were never still. For a man presumed to be wealthy, he was wearing an extraordinary suit, one of those green things that made him look like a cheap sport, with a pink tie that swore loudly at the suit. All in all, he was far from an imposing figure.

It was not until Currie had told him who Bartley was, that he showed the slightest sign of interest in either of us, and even then his manner was far from cordial. You could see, in fact, that he was wondering why Bartley had come and wishing him a thousand miles away.

Bartley himself, seeing how Slyke felt, said with a friendly laugh, "It's hardly right to run in on you this way, Mr. Slyke. I was coming over to see you formally in the morning; but as Mr. Currie said he had some business with you this afternoon, I decided to come with him."

He then told Slyke why we had come to Circle Lake. The man made no response to this, nor did he say anything when Bartley told him of the Governor's interest in the two men now in prison for the burglary.

When Bartley had finished, he actually snarled, "I am sick of the whole thing. Those men had a fair trial and were found guilty. What more do you want?"

Bartley, whose eyes had never left his face, though Slyke refused to meet them, shot out suddenly, "But you were never sure that they were guilty."

The remark was so unexpected that Slyke's face grew red and he stammered, "But—well— anyway they were— proven guilty."

"But you yourself said that you could not identify them."

The servant who had ushered us in, passed through the room at this moment, and Slyke glanced at him as if he would have liked to order him to show us the door. If we had been alone he might have yielded, but Currie's presence saved us.

"That may be so, but there were others that did recognize them, even though I could not," he answered.

As Slyke was getting angrier and angrier, Bartley changed his tactics. When he sets out to win a person, there are few that can resist him; and in a moment or two even Slyke thawed under his smile.

"I can understand," Bartley remarked, "how bored you must be with the whole affair. There must be so many curious people always coming around. As you probably know, Mr. Slyke, there is a growing feeling that those men in prison are innocent. What I am to do is to find out whether there is any ground for such a feeling. I know that you will be the very first person to wish them pardoned if they are innocent. Can I come over tomorrow morning and have a talk with you about the burglary? My wide experience may help me to see things that the others have overlooked. The Governor asked me to look into the matter, you know."

Slyke did not seem over pleased at this suggestion, and muttered that he was going fishing in the morning. He finally agreed that his step daughter Ruth could give Bartley whatever information he wanted. After all, she was the one who had recognized one of the men. Seeing that so far as he was concerned, the conversation was over we took our leave.

As we re-entered the woods, Bartley remarked with a laugh, "He was not what you might call keen to see us. That burglary for some reason seems to be a sore subject with him."

When we arrived at the house, Currie excused himself to see about some matters on the estate, and we went up to our rooms. Bartley found a chair near the window, and taking a book from his bag, began to read. I glanced over his shoulder to see what the yellow covered book might be, but the title had no significance for me, "*La Gentille Andalouse*" by Francisco Delicado. It was a romance of sixteenth century Spain, Bartley informed me, seeing my curious glance.

As I did not care to read myself, I went to the other window, drew up a chair, and lighted my pipe. For a while I watched the clouds that were drifting over the mountains. Then I looked down at the calm surface of the

lake where a few men were fishing in small boats, and
still nearer at hand where Currie was talking to one of
his farm hands. The next thing I knew Bartley was
shaking me back to consciousness; I had fallen asleep.

Currie had said that if we came down in evening dress
he would throw us out; so still in white flannels, we
joined him in the dining-room. He was talking with a
young man of about thirty five, whom he introduced as
Doctor King. The doctor was a book fan, so Currie told
Bartley, adding that he suspected that he knew more
about books even than he did about medicine.

We laughed at this and shook hands with the doctor.
He was a likable sort of a chap, with clean shaven face,
tanned red by outdoor life, and dark blue eyes with a
twinkle in them. Upon his coat was the little insignia
that showed he had seen service. A closer glance revealed
that the doctor's nerves were bad; his hands twitched,
and all during the evening I noticed that every noise
startled him. Once in a while, too, he seemed to find it
difficult to remember the word he wanted to use. We
learned later that he had been shell shocked.

The doctor was delighted to meet Bartley. "I have
read that book of yours on rare poisons many times, Mr.
Bartley. I have even read your little book on Casanova."

Bartley laughed. "You are one of the few men that
have ever read it."

Currie had promised us a good dinner, and we were
not disappointed. The doctor showed himself to be as well
read as Bartley, who is interested in anything that is a
book. Though he reads poetry, and once in a while a
novel, his interest lies deeper than these. Religions,
especially those that throw light on primitive religious
beliefs, anthropology, science, medicine, are what he
enjoys most. He often says that the accounts of the crimes
and the sins of the past tell more about the real life of
people than all the histories that have ever been written.
As the dinner progressed, we found that the doctor was

also interested in these subjects, and Bartley and he found many a congenial topic.

Their discussion finally settled down upon the two schools of psycho analysis. From the first, this talk bored Currie; and every once in a while he would throw me an appealing glance. At last the conversation returned to crime, and Currie suddenly asked Bartley if it had ever been discovered who Jack the Ripper was.

What made him ask the question I do not know. Bartley replied that though no name had ever been given out, Scotland Yard had come to the conclusion that the crimes had been committed either by a crazy Polish Jew, or more probably by a doctor. A well known doctor had been on the border line of insanity at the time the Whitechapel murders had occurred; and when he dropped out of sight the murders ceased. The English detectives were almost positive that he was the murderer, but they could not prove it.

"No more than they were able to prove," Currie interrupted, "that those men they sent to jail ever broke into Slyke's house."

The doctor remarked, "I was called in as the family physician by Slyke, on the night of the burglary. He told me, at the time, that he had not recognized either of the men."

Bartley did not speak, but sat watching the glowing tip of his cigarette. I knew he was waiting for the doctor to say more.

"Both the men that were arrested," the doctor continued, "had worked at one time or another for Slyke. You would have thought that, if they had been the ones who broke into his house, he would have recognized them. But he told me positively that night, or rather that morning, that he had not recognized either of them."

As the doctor did not continue, Bartley asked, "Then he never, at any time, said he recognized either of the men?"

The doctor shook his head. "No, he never did. At the trial he said there had not been enough light for him to see their faces. Ruth, the step daughter, was the only one who thought she recognized them—that is, one of them."

Bartley made no comment, but I saw him smile to himself. King, who seemed to be willing to talk, went on: "It was about three o'clock in the morning when they 'phoned me. The only injury that Slyke had received was a nervous shock. I did not see the girl or any other member of the family. As far as I could discern, nothing had been disturbed in the living room."

Currie broke in with, "How do you and Miss Potter get along?"

The doctor laughed and threw out his hands. Seeing that we did not understand the joke, he explained, "Miss Potter is a sister of Slyke's dead wife, and runs the house for him. Her temper is, to say the least, sudden. Besides, she is a very ardent spiritualist."

Currie gave a groan at the last remark, and said in a humorous voice, "John, that old dame is always having dreams and runs a Ouija board. You'd think to hear her that the board can do everything but get the meals. The other day she said to me, 'My dear Mr. Currie, do you believe in spirits?' And I said, 'Sure, if they are bottled.' She called me a skeptic or something of the kind."

When the laughter had died away, Bartley asked the doctor quietly, "What was the mix up between the state police and the local police?"

King looked surprised. "Why, I never knew there was any. Of course, there is some foolish jealousy between the two branches. The arrest of the men by the state troopers may have increased it a bit. But the state police arrested those men simply because they were sneaking through the fields at three o'clock in the morning and refused to give an account of themselves. I have heard that the officer in command of the troopers never believed that those men had anything to do with the Slyke affair. Most of the evidence against them was not found until several days later—some by the local police and some by Slyke's chauffeur. When the police were first called in, they didn't find any evidence; indeed, I do not think they looked for any until the next morning."

Currie rose and suggested we play a game of billiards; and the conversation about the burglary ended. While I play at the game, Bartley plays with uncanny skill, and both Currie and the doctor were almost equally good players. It was not until some hours later, when the doctor was called away by telephone, that we realized how late it was.

Bartley and I were tired after our ride and the long hours of visiting, and we went immediately to our rooms. Neither was inclined to talk, but Bartley did unburden himself enough to say he believed that Slyke knew who had committed the burglary but for some reason wanted to hide the fact. Five minutes later, I was in bed and asleep.

I slept without dreaming, until someone aroused me by a vigorous shake. For a second, I thought I had just gotten into bed, then I opened my eyes and saw that the first rays of the sun were coming in the window. Bending over me, already dressed, was Bartley. I vaguely noticed a strange look in his eyes and traces of excitement on his face, but I was too tired to be interested and started to turn over and go to sleep again. He threw the covers off me, saying in an eager voice:

"Get up, Pelt, get up quick! Dr. King has just 'phoned us to meet him at Slyke's house."

Why should King want to see us at such an early hour in the morning, and above all at Slyke's? Bartley's next words brought me wide awake with all desire for sleep gone. With a curious note in his voice, he added, "They found Slyke in his bed—" he paused, "—dead."

"Dead?" I questioned. "But why—how—"

Bartley did not wait for me to finish. "Shot. They told King it was suicide."

III. Suicide Or Murder

I WAS out of bed in a moment, and getting into my clothes as rapidly as I could. What Bartley had told me seemed almost incredible. Why, only a few hours before we had seen and talked with Slyke. He had not acted like a man in trouble, yet he had killed himself! I could tell by his grave manner that Bartley thought this a very serious matter.

Fully dressed, I followed him out onto the lawn which was still wet with the morning dew. We crossed the field and went through the woods in silence. At last I ventured to ask what it was that he had heard regarding Slyke's death.

"About five minutes before I woke you, King 'phoned to say that he had been called to Slyke's house—that he was dead. He was told that he had committed suicide. He asked us to join him in front of the house as soon as possible."

The woods were filled with the songs of birds greeting the new day, and this, with the peacefulness of the morning, contrasted so strongly with the horror we were expecting to find when we reached Slyke's house, that I became greatly depressed.

"Why should he have killed himself?" I asked. "He did not look to me like a man who had nerve enough for that."

In a moody tone Bartley replied, "I don't think he did," and left me to puzzle out his meaning.

When we reached the house there was no outward evidence that anything unusual had taken place. As we approached, I noticed at the back of the house a white curtain napping back and forth in an open window of the tower. Signs of life there were none. Doctor King's car was coming up the drive as we neared the front of the house. With him was a short, red faced Irishman in police uniform, whom he introduced, a moment later, as Roche, the chief of the local police force.

He was one of those talkative individuals to whom an official position gives an exalted idea of their own importance. He bowed, mopped his face with his handkerchief, then said, "I am very pleased to meet you, gentlemen. Your name, Mr. Bartley, I have heard many times. But there won't be any chance for you to show your skill here today. From what I am told, the poor man killed himself."

Paying little attention to Roche, Bartley turned to the doctor. "Just what did they tell you over the 'phone?" he asked.

"Only what I told you. I had just gotten out of bed, when the bell rang and an excited voice asked me to come at once, as they had just found Slyke dead and thought he had killed himself."

Before we could ring, in fact before we could reach the top step of the piazza, the door was flung open and a woman of about fifty rushed wildly to the doctor's side. She was far from an attractive woman, thin, with what is called a hatchet face. Her dress was carelessly fastened and several buttons showed. She incessantly brushed stray locks of uncombed grayish hair from her eyes, in which fear and excitement showed. Her shrill voice broke as she grabbed the doctor's arm and cried:

"It's come, doctor, it's come just as I expected. He's killed himself. Oh, I knew there would be trouble. Night after night I have had a message on the Ouija board. It said again and again, 'Trouble, trouble coming.' And I have dreamed that he was dead, too. It's come. He is dead."

Bartley gave me a look. Evidently this was the woman of whom the doctor had told us, the sister of Slyke's dead wife and an ardent spiritualist. One needed only a glance at her to see that she was the kind of a woman that will believe in such messages, nervous and impressionable.

It was some time before the doctor could get her calmed down enough to introduce us. She showed no surprise at Bartley being present; I doubt if she had ever heard of him.

By the time the introductions had been completed, we were all in the big room in which we had met Slyke the day before. Currie had told us the previous evening that Slyke was to have a card party that night, and the room showed that there had been one. In the center were three card tables, with the chairs pushed back from them, evidently left as they were when the party broke up. Upon the tables the cards lay in scrambled heaps, and ash trays with cigar butts were all over the room. The air had that musty odor that hangs to a place where men have been smoking heavily and have forgotten to open the windows.

After a quick glance around, Bartley turned to Miss Potter. "Suppose you tell us how Mr. Slyke was discovered."

She gave a start, wrung her hands, and answered excitedly, "The butler found him. Mr. Slyke was going fishing today, and was to have been called early. The butler went to knock on his door and found it half opened and—"

Bartley interrupted, "Then, I take it, he usually kept the door of his room locked."

"He did. I do not know why. The butler saw it was open, looked in, called him, and got no answer. Then he came and told me. I was at breakfast. I went to his room, and there he was—" and her voice trailed off in horror.

For a second or two no one moved or spoke. I could see what a shock the discovery of the body had been to this woman. No wonder she was nervous. Indeed, for some reason we all seemed rather uneasy.

Bartley's face was very grave as he said, "What did you do when you found he was dead?"

For the hundredth time she brushed the hair from her eyes. "I called the servants—Ruth was not here. Then I telephoned for the doctor."

Roche did not like Bartley's doing all the questioning, and he asserted his official position by saying that it was time we went up to the room where Slyke lay. Miss Potter led the way, walking like one weary and overwhelmed with grief. The stairs at the landing separated to the right and left, each ending in a long hall. At the landing the walls of the tower made almost another house within a house. The woman entered a half opened doorway, and we followed close at her heels.

The room, thirty feet square, was larger than I had expected to find. It was furnished like a den. The bed in one corner was the only evidence that it was used for sleeping purposes. A couple of arm chairs, a few smaller chairs, a large flat top desk, and several book cases, almost empty, completed the furnishings. The few pictures were mostly copies of old English sporting scenes, with here and there a poor nude. In the left hand corner of the room a pair of stairs ran to the floor above. But we paid little attention to these things; our thoughts were centered upon the bed. Under the white coverlet we could see the still form of a man huddled in a heap, lying on his back, his legs extending into the air a little beyond the foot of the bed. His face was half hidden by the bed clothes which were closely drawn around his neck and over his chin. The doctor had taken his position at Slyke's head, and we all stood about him in silence until Bartley's voice broke the stillness.

"Miss Potter, when you came in, did you touch the bed clothes at all?"

She hesitated a second, as if trying to think, then replied, "No, I gave a quick look, saw he was dead, and hurried from the room."

"And they are just as you found them—I mean, up around his chin this way?"

" So far as I know. The butler says he never went near the bed at all."

Without a word, Bartley pulled back the covers as far as the man's chest. Slyke's nightshirt had not been buttoned. His face was calm, showing not the slightest sign of a death struggle; his eyes closed; his mouth partly open. As Bartley pulled the clothes still further down, we saw that his right hand held a revolver. Then we noticed the wound that had caused his death. It was under his left ear, half hidden by the pillow, on which were a few drops of blood.

The doctor knelt and examined the wound closely, then rose to his feet. Bartley in turn bent over the body, but he turned his attention to the hand holding the revolver. It lay close to the side of the body with the fingers gripping the butt firmly. Bartley moved it a little, but did not attempt to loosen their clutch. With another glance at the pillow and the face upon it, he rose, his lips compressed, his face grave.

Roche turned to us with a half smile. "It's such a simple case, Mr. Bartley, that it won't need any of your skill to solve it. The doctor won't need to hold a long inquest. It's as clear a case of suicide as I have ever seen. He undressed, got in bed, and then shot himself. There is the gun in his hand. Not much in this case, is there?"

The doctor half nodded in agreement; but Bartley, as if he had not heard, bent again over the bed, his face stern, and examined the revolver. When he straightened up, he said simply. "It's serious enough, Chief. Murder always is, and this is murder."

At his words Miss Potter, who had been standing beside me, eagerly watching everything that was done, gave a little cry. As for myself, I was not greatly surprised at his words. His manner had been so serious that I had been expecting something of the sort. Roche grunted in amusement, and turned to King.

"Do you hear the man now! Murder! Why, that's foolish, Mr. Bartley. It's suicide. He has the gun in his hand."

Bartley gave him an amused glance as he answered, "It may be foolish, but it's murder. True, he has the gun in his hand; and that makes it look something like suicide, I agree; but that's just what someone wanted us to think."

This statement seemed to make Roche angry. He may not have liked to have his opinion challenged, or he may have resented the way Bartley was taking the lead. His face flushed and he sneered, "Oh, come now, how do you expect to prove that?"

Bartley did not answer but simply pointed to the gun. I think we all looked at it rather foolishly, as if we expected to find in it, by some miracle, a clue to his statement.

As we did not speak, he replied, "Roche, you think that the fact he is found dead with the gun in his hand, proves that he committed suicide. But to me, that gun and the way it is held, proves murder. Not only murder, but that the gun was placed in his hand after death. Look at the way the hand grasps the revolver. It is not held so firmly but that with some effort it can be removed. The testimony of all medico legalists is that in cases of suicide or of accidents, the attitudes and acts of the person whose life is suddenly ended are continued for some seconds after death."

Roche was listening attentively, but Bartley's last words were a little over his head. Perceiving that he did not understand, Bartley explained at greater length:

"What I mean by that is simply this: In cases of suicide or where a man shoots himself by accident and dies suddenly, the hand clutches the weapon so tightly that after death it is almost impossible to loosen his grip. There is a muscular spasm that follows death which causes the hand to grip the weapon even more tightly than in life. Most medico legal books agree that a weapon so held is the best evidence of suicide."

He glanced at the doctor, who nodded in response, yet glanced down in a puzzled way at the hand holding the gun.

"The strength of the grip is only a question of degree. Lacassagne, a French doctor, after hundreds of tests, proved that a man can be murdered and the weapon placed in his hand after death, but that the grasp will not be as firm as it would have been if he had shot himself. In Slyke's case, if he had fired the shot that killed him, the muscular reaction would be such that I ought to be able to move the gun only with a great effort. As it moves easily, I believe the revolver was placed in his hand after death and the fingers forced around it. As the death rigor increased, the grip became more secure. I say again, someone placed the revolver in his hand after he was killed, wishing us to believe it was suicide."

Roche was not willing to accept this statement. "That's a fine theory," he sneered. "Just the sort of a thing you city detectives dig up. You have got to have more than that to make me think he was murdered."

Bartley gave a little shrug of his shoulders, as if bored by the whole thing. "As you wish! I had an idea you might want more evidence than that." He paused, and we waited breathlessly for his next words.

"Look at his eyes. They are tightly closed. It is a recognized fact by all medical men that, when death comes by violence, the eyes of the victim are wide open and staring. On the other hand, in cases where death comes slowly, they may be half shut. In neither instance are they ever fully closed. "When we find a case where the eyes are tightly closed, we know that someone has closed them, and that it was done after the man was dead."

I think that each of us noticed for the first time Slyke's eyes. He continued:

"Here we find the eyes closed. If he committed suicide, they would be open. If he had been murdered, they would be open also. Though the fact they are closed does not help us to decide between murder and suicide, it does point to the fact that someone has been in the room and closed them after he died. May we not suppose that the same person that placed the gun in his hand to make his death appear to be suicide, was also the one who closed his eyes, not knowing that they should have remained open, no matter how he died?"

Again he paused, as if waiting for someone to speak, then as no one did, he continued:

"But that is not all, Roche. You should use your common sense. Here is Slyke, dead, with both hands by his sides, and the bed clothes up around his neck and over his chin. You don't expect me to believe that he could have shot himself, pulled the clothes around his neck, and then placed his arms by his sides. He did not have time enough for that; he died instantly, without even a struggle. A second after the shot was fired, this world was over as far as he was concerned. It was someone else who arranged those things. Someone who wished his death to appear to be suicide, and in trying to do that rather overdid the whole thing. No, I do not think there is the slightest doubt in the world but that he was murdered."

Roche had long since lost his confident air; in fact, more than once his face had flushed at Bartley's tone. He said nothing, though, even when Bartley had finished. The doctor, too, had listened with interest, yet I was not altogether sure that he wholly agreed with Bartley's reasoning.

He now asked, "Could it not have been suicide after all; and the closing of the eyes and the arrangement of the bed clothes have been done by the person who discovered the body?"

Bartley admitted that there was a faint possibility that such a thing might have happened, but added that the chances were against it.

"But, if Slyke was murdered," the doctor asked, "why should all this trouble have been taken to make it look like suicide?"

Bartley, who was bending over the bed examining the body, did not answer until he straightened up again.

"King," he said in a grave voice, "I am sure this is murder, not suicide. The person who killed him wished us to believe he killed himself. I have an idea that he forgot how a body should look after death, and the very things he used to make us think Slyke killed himself, prove to me that he was murdered. Moreover, he was not killed in bed."

Both the doctor and Roche looked as if this last statement were too unbelievable; and even I, who had long since ceased to be surprised at anything that Bartley might say, wondered a little.

"When you look at the pillow," he explained, "on which his head lies, you will find only one or two spots of blood. The shirt, in fact, has none at all. The wound must have bled some— not much, it is true, but far more than it seems to have done from the appearance of the bed. He was killed elsewhere and placed in this bed afterwards. I doubt if he was even undressed at the time of his death."

This statement seemed incredible; and I could understand the little laugh that Roche gave as he responded, "Oh, come, Mr. Bartley, that's going too far. I am willing to admit that you may be right when you say that he was murdered. But to ask us to believe that by simply looking at the bed you can tell that he was placed on it after his death and that he was dressed at the moment when he was killed, is a little too much."

Before Bartley could answer, Miss Potter, who had remained silent although obviously very nervous, asked if she might go to her room and leave the doctor in charge. This delegating of her authority to the doctor did not appeal to Roche; and he told her that, if her brother in law had been murdered, it would be the police and not the doctor who would take charge of things. The ordeal through which she had passed must have been more than she could stand, for she made no comment on his challenge but started to leave the room.

"Miss Potter," Bartley asked, as she reached the door, "did you ever see this revolver in Mr. Slyke's hand?"

She hesitated a moment and then replied, "It's Mr. Slyke's; he was in the habit of keeping it in a drawer of his desk. The gun was bought soon after the burglary, but, so far as I know, he has never used it."

Although her statement that the revolver had belonged to the dead man made the suicide theory plausible, yet I could not quite see how the facts that Bartley had brought forward to disprove the suicide could be overthrown.

When she had left the room, Bartley turned to Roche with an amused smile upon his lips but with the little glint in his eyes that he always has when aroused.

"Roche, I am perfectly willing to let you take charge of the case. It's your duty, not mine. But I, too, am working on a matter that concerns the dead man. It may even be mixed up in this. Why not work together, you along your line, I along mine? I won't take any of the credit away from you. I have had far more experience in cases of this kind than you have had, and I have an idea that both of us will need all the help we can get before we are through with it. So why not start on friendly terms and do what has to be done together?"

Roche brightened. I could see that all he wanted was that his official position as chief of the local police be recognized; for, like all small town police chiefs, he had a rather absurd idea of its importance. He was beginning to realize that he was confronted by no ordinary case and that, instead of being able to solve it alone, he would need all the expert assistance he could get. As this knowledge dawned on him, he became at once more agreeable.

"What makes you think, Mr. Bartley," he asked, "that Slyke was dressed at the time he was killed?"

Bartley answered, "If Slyke had been killed in bed there would have been more blood on the bed clothes than the few drops we see on the pillow. His nightshirt, too, if it had been worn at the time he was killed, would have had some traces of blood on it. There are no such stains. This, and the fact that death must have been instantaneous, makes me feel sure that he was undressed after he was killed and then placed on the bed in the position in which we have found him."

Bartley began a search of the room, using a small glass once or twice as if he were looking for finger prints. Slyke's clothes were flung over a chair, and one of his stockings had fallen to the floor. The way the gray suit lay on the chair made me wonder if Bartley was right when he said the murderer had undressed him after the crime. It looked so much as if it had been carelessly flung there by a man preparing for bed.

After going through Slyke's pockets Bartley said slowly, "I have grave doubts if he was even killed in this room."

This statement startled us more than anything else he had yet said. I saw a look of doubt come into the doctor's face as he glanced at Roche, who seemed even more skeptical. I myself wondered why Bartley made the remark, although I knew he was not given to wild statements. He continued to examine the room, searching the floor, looking into the drawers of the desk, examining the walls even; then he came back to the clothing.

Picking up the blue silk shirt from the chair, he examined it a second time before he said, "I was right. He was not killed in this room. Here is the suit he wore. You will notice that all his clothing is placed on this chair in the manner that a man would naturally place it if he was undressing for bed. But there is no button in the front of his shirt to hold his collar, and one stocking is missing; Any man may lose a collar button, but if he does that button will be dropped at the place where he undressed. No button is in this room. It was lost in the room in which he was undressed. We find his shoes here but only one stocking, and we naturally ask where is the other stocking. Then, too, there are no blood stains anywhere in this room. Though his wound did not bleed much, it must have bled some. These are the reasons why I say he was not killed in this room, or even undressed here."

His explanation seemed reasonable enough, yet somewhat mystifying. Why had the murderer taken all this trouble to undress Slyke, and why had he done it in some other room? The next question was just as puzzling. If Slyke had not been killed in this room, where had the crime taken place? As if he had read my thoughts, Roche suggested that as there was another room in the tower, we might see what could be found there.

The butler, who entered at this moment, did his best not to glance at the bed. He was holding with great difficulty a half grown Airedale that growled fiercely when he saw us. The butler motioned to the doctor to come to him. As he reached his side, Doctor King placed his hand upon the dog's head and it ceased to show its teeth and licked his fingers. For several moments he and the butler held a low conversation, then King turned to us to say that he had just been called to the hospital for an operation and would have to leave at once.

Bartley scribbled something on a piece of paper, and handing it to the doctor said, "I think there ought to be a picture taken of the body so it can be used at the inquest."

The doctor agreed and went out, accompanied by the butler. As the door closed behind them Bartley went to lock it but the key was missing. After a moment's hesitation he decided it would do no harm to leave it unlocked while we were gone, and we all started for the floor above.

The room we entered was of the same size as the one in which we had found Slyke. Here, too, there was little furniture—three chairs grouped around a little table in the center of the room, a lounge in one corner, a small desk in another. It was the table that attracted Bartley's attention. On it stood a half emptied bottle of Scotch whiskey, and beside the bottle three glasses, one of them holding about a spoonful of liquor. Near one of the glasses was a half smoked cigarette and a magazine, and on the opposite side of the table the stub of a cigar. Bartley looked at both of them with keen interest and finally placed them in an envelope. The cigarette must have been a very high priced one, for the end was of the finest straw. The appearance of the table suggested that three men had been present and that two of them had been smoking. A conference, perhaps, at which a bottle of whiskey had assisted. Aside from the table, there seemed to be nothing of interest in the room.

While Bartley was still glancing at the table, I walked over to the large window and drew aside the heavy curtain that reached to the floor. At my feet was a playing card that had been concealed by its folds. Glancing around to see if there were any others and finding none, I brought the card to Bartley.

As I stepped to his side, I saw that he was examining the magazine. Since it was a current number, I had not paid any attention to it, but he was studying its back cover with great care. Like many magazines, the back carried a gaudy advertisement that covered the entire page. This one was for a brand of cheap cigarettes and had an unusual amount of unused white space. Bartley pointed silently to where someone had idly amused himself by drawing on it with a pencil, a habit many people have. The design was simple, only a mass of scrolls, with a little figure here and there, and lines running through them.

"Whatever it meant to Bartley, the mass of zeros held no significance to me. He did not enlighten me, but placed the magazine in his pocket. Then I showed him the playing card and told him where I found it. He asked, "Are there no more?" I was answering, "No," when Roche interrupted, "Yes, there is one."

He pointed to the stairway that led to the top of the tower. There, lying under the bottom step, was a second playing card with the same design on the back as the one I had found. What were they doing in that room? Bartley smiled to himself as he examined the second card.

Roche asked, "What do they mean?"

With a gesture that might have meant anything, it was so expressive, Bartley replied, "They had a card party downstairs last night."

Roche was excited in a moment. "I'll tell you what it means. Someone at that party killed Slyke, followed him up here and killed him."

It was not a half bad theory, and even Bartley did not protest as much as I had thought he would. Instead he said, "There is something in what you say, Roche. We must look first for the person who had the chance to kill him. You assume that after the party the person who dropped these cards did what any absent-minded person might do. That is, he placed the cards of his last hand in his pocket. He may have followed Slyke up here, hidden behind the curtain, and as he killed him dropped some of his cards on the floor."

He paused, half frowned, as if the theory did not quite appeal to him and added slowly, "Still, Roche, there are other things to be considered. Those two cards are in different parts of the room; not together as we might have expected if they had been dropped by accident. It looks to me as if they might have been placed where we found them by design."

"Design?" questioned Roche, not understanding.

"Yes, design. As if some one wished us to think just what you thought. Then there is that bottle of whiskey and the three glasses. You might assume that instead of there having been two persons in this room there were three."

"Three?" we both queried.

"Yes, three. You might even carry the theory so far as to say that one of them might have been behind the curtain, while Slyke and the other one were seated at the table. That drives you up against another proposition, however. All three glasses have been drunk from. The glasses show that they were all used at about the same time. Evidently two of the men smoked; the third did not. What I wonder is, were these three persons in the room at one and the same time?"

Roche, who had long since lost his air of self satisfaction, now offered to help us make a thorough examination of the room. When we had ended our unsuccessful search, Bartley stood silent, a puzzled expression on his face.

"It's more mysterious than ever," he said at last. "I am sure he was not killed in the room below. I am also sure he was not killed here. There must be blood spots somewhere, yet where? There are none in this room."

He went to the window and glanced out, then came back and glanced up at the steps that led to the roof. All at once his face brightened, and motioning us to follow him he bounded up the seven steps to the little door that opened onto the balcony. We followed more slowly.

We found ourselves on a balcony some four feet wide that ran around the tower. About eight or ten feet below its bronze tipped top, an iron railing protected the edge of the balcony and was covered with ivy, as were also the sides of the tower itself. For a moment we all paused and looked at the wonderful view. The sun was now high, and the mountains to the north were a misty blue. Near at hand the lake was covered with a faint haze like a cloud of thin cigarette smoke. Below us, on the estate of the dead man, not a soul was in sight. Even Bartley paused for a moment, standing with his hand on the rail, his face serious, his eyes thoughtful. But it was for a moment only; the next he was out of sight around the tower. Almost instantly we heard him call us, and when we reached his side he was on his knees examining the floor and the lower part of the wall. Looking where he pointed, I saw at his feet a dark splotch on the floor of the balcony, and a little higher up several similar spots on the wall of the tower. I realized that, at last, he had found what he had been looking for.

That this discovery puzzled him, I knew; but I also knew that it had not surprised him. One of his favorite maxims was: when you make up your mind a thing is impossible, sit back and watch it take place. There was no doubt that the splotches we saw were blood, and that it had been shed within a few hours. Had he expected to find them just where he did, I wondered.

As if answering my thoughts, he said, "Yes, Slyke was murdered here."

Though I had been sure he would say that, it did not seem reasonable that any person should select the balcony of a tower, fifty or more feet in the air, as a place in which to commit a murder. It became still more puzzling when I remembered that Slyke had been carried down two flights of stairs, undressed, placed in bed and a revolver clasped in his hand. Roche, his fat face puzzled, gave me a bewildered glance. I could sympathize with his astonishment as I felt much the same way myself.

I expressed my surprise to Bartley and he responded, "I know, Pelt, all that you have said and all that you are thinking. It does seem out of all reason that anyone should pick the top of this tower for a murder. Yet here are the spots of blood, and there are none anywhere else. These spots are not over seven hours old; you can tell that by the way they have dried. I am sure he was not killed downstairs; it must have been here, and "

He paused and, bending over, picked something up. At first I could not make out what it was; then I saw that it was a gold plated collar button such as a man wears in the front of his shirt. Roche needed only one look to identify it, "Slyke's!"

Bartley did not speak until he had walked entirely around the tower and was again beside us.

"Chief," he said, "we may say there is now no doubt that Slyke was killed up here. I do not know why such a strange place was chosen, but I do know that he was dragged down these stairs after his death and placed in his bed to make his death appear to be suicide. The odds were very much in favor of the criminal's being able to succeed in his design, too. But he slipped up—slipped up in the manner in which he put the gun in the hand and in the way in which he closed the eyes. But why he should have killed Slyke up here I cannot understand."

Roche, no longer suspicious and jealous of his authority as a police officer, showed his admiration openly. "Well, Mr. Bartley, it's beyond me. I could never have found it out myself. But we have a lot more yet to find out."

Bartley agreed, and added that at least we knew that it was murder and not suicide, and where the crime had been committed.

As I looked at the splotches of blood, I wondered if, after all, it would not require more than these to prove that Slyke had been murdered on the spot on which we stood. Bartley read my doubts in my face and half smiled.

"There are more than the stains, Pelt. The only way to understand a crime is to see it as a whole. Now the balcony is the only place where we have found any evidence at all. Let us try to build up the picture."

He paused for a moment, as if thinking, then continued, "Slyke gave a party last evening. The crime must have been committed after the party broke up. That was probably between one and two o'clock in the morning. One man, perhaps two, stayed behind to talk with Slyke. We can't say positively that they did, but they may have. Roche thinks that this man, or men, committed the murder. One man may have stayed and then gone away before the murder, or someone else may have come later. They may have come up here to see the view, and one of them shot him. After the crime the body, at any rate, was taken downstairs again and undressed, the nightshirt placed on it, and it laid in bed. As he wanted it to appear like suicide, the murderer placed the gun in the dead man's fingers, but he either did not remember, or perhaps did not know, how the eyes should look after a sudden death. The very things done to make us think it was suicide prove that it could not have possibly been one."

Again I looked down at the spots of blood, wondering if they were enough to prove that the crime had really been committed on this lower balcony. Bartley, seeing my glance, added, "Go around the tower, Pelt, and you will see how every few feet there are little drops of dried blood, showing that the body was taken around to the darkest side of the tower after the murder. There was a moon last night, as you know. You will find also that, beginning here, the ivy has been broken and torn as if some heavy object had been brushed against it."

Doing as he suggested, I found that the ivy at the top and on the inside of the rail had been broken in many places and was hanging down. It looked as if some heavy object had indeed been dragged past it, such a heavy object as Slyke's body might have been.

As Bartley was now ready to go downstairs again, we all returned to the room below. The first thing we saw when we entered, was a brown stocking, the mate to the one in the room below. We had not noticed it on our way to the balcony as it lay half under the rug, and the opened door hid it. Bartley picked it up, glanced at it, smiled, and was going to say something when a voice called to us from below.

In a second we were down the stairs and in Slyke's bedroom. The door to the stairway was closed just as we had left it; Bartley opened it to find a young man with a big camera under his arm on the landing. He gave us an inquiring glance; then seeing Roche, whom he seemed to know, announced, "Doctor King said you wanted me up here to take some pictures."

Bartley explained to the young man the type of pictures that would be needed for the inquest and, though he had never done any work of this kind before, he grasped at once what was required. He asked no useless questions, but when Bartley had finished his instructions, inquired, "What shall I take first?"

Bartley glanced at the bed and I thought gave a slight start. The bed clothes that had been drawn down around Slyke's waist when we were examining the revolver in his hand, had been replaced by Bartley, before we went to the floor above, "in the position in which they were when we entered the room—that is, around Slyke's neck and half covering his chin.

"You had better take first a picture of the bed as it is now," Bartley suggested. "Then I will pull the bed clothes down and you can take a picture of his hand with the revolver in it."

The first picture took some time, for the young man could not seem to find the proper place for his camera, but at last it was done.

"Now for the other one." Bartley went to the side of the bed, reached down, and pulled back the bed clothes. As he drew them down he paused and a cry escaped him.

"Look!"

As my eyes fell on the hand of the dead man I, too, started. When we had gone up stairs the revolver was clasped in Slyke's still fingers. Now they were empty. Someone had removed the gun!

IV. THE DEAD MAN'S EYES

FOR several moments we were all so startled that none of us spoke. For myself, I could only look at the hand that had, so short a time before, held the revolver. I could not imagine who could have taken it, and what his purpose in doing so could be. I glanced at Bartley. His face was set, a white line showing around his tightly closed lips. He was angry, very angry. Only twice had I seen him so angry, and both times it had been with men who were cruelly mistreating a dog. No matter what unexpected situation arose, he usually remained good natured.

As he turned to Roche, who stood with eyes bulging, his voice shook a little. "Roche, go and get Miss Potter at once. Tell her to call all the servants and have them assemble in the living room. I will be down in a moment."

Roche hurried out without speaking. Immediately Bartley bent again over the bed, studying the position of the hand that had held the revolver. When he straightened up he told the photographer that he would not need him any longer. As soon as the young man had left the room, Bartley turned to me with a rueful little smile.

"Well, Pelt, I certainly slipped up this morning. I was never so angry with myself as I was a moment ago."

"Why?" I asked.

He looked at me as if he wondered that I should ask so absurd a question. "You ought to know. We left this room without locking the door. True, there was no key, but I should have left either Roche or you on guard. Instead of that we have given some one a chance to slip in here and remove the revolver. He thought he was removing a valuable piece of evidence. The joke is that the removal of the revolver does not make much difference. We all saw the gun, and we all heard Miss Potter say that it had belonged to Slyke."

"But," I asked, "who could have known about it—I mean that it was murder? You were the only one who suggested it. Every one else who knew about the crime thought that it was suicide. At least, that's what Doctor King said he was told over the 'phone."

I received a curious look from Bartley. who waited for some time before he responded, "That's the queer thing about it, Pelt. Only those that were in the room with us are presumed to know it is murder. That is, unless Miss Potter told others when she left here. She might have told the butler, for instance. The strange thing is that it was first made to appear to be suicide by placing the gun in Slyke's hand. Now that evidence is removed I hardly know what we are expected to believe. I had an idea, even before we came into this room, that Miss Potter knew that her brother-in law had been murdered."

What more he might have said I do not know, for at that moment Roche returned. He looked sheepish and rather ill at ease. He told us that Miss Potter had refused to call the servants, saying that Bartley had no authority to compel her to do so, and—he paused a moment, his red face flushing a deeper red—she had added that she considered Roche was the only one who had any authority to give orders here. For herself, she was convinced that Slyke had committed suicide, and that Bartley did not know what he was talking about when he said that he had been murdered.

Bartley looked very much astonished as Roche reported her words, then gave a low whistle.

"Does that satisfy you, Roche?" he asked.

"No, it doesn't," Roche replied, shaking his head vigorously. "It doesn't, not by one little bit. I am frank enough to say, Mr. Bartley, that though I don't see any light in this all, I know you can. Your experience and reputation are both greater than mine. I am, of course, the head of the local police and shall have to put up some kind of a bluff, but I wish you would take charge of the case. I don't know just where your pay will come from, though."

Bartley was silent, his face thoughtful; when he spoke he made no reference to what Roche had just said.

"You say Miss Potter doesn't wish to give us any aid at all?"

Roche nodded.

"Well, then, Roche, we will have to go down and see what we can do with her together. You tell her I am your assistant. You might also add that if she refuses to give us the information we need, we can arrest her on the charge of obstructing an officer in the discharge of his duty."

Both men grinned at this, and, still smiling, Roche led the way from the room. From the top of the stairs we could see Miss Potter in the living room below, pacing nervously back and forth. When she heard us descending, with Roche in the lead, she stopped at the desk and began to arrange its contents in an effort to cover her nervousness and confusion. She did not look up even when we were at her side.

After waiting for her to speak, Bartley said in a grave tone, "Miss Potter, I understand that you told Officer Roche that you refused to call the servants."

She raised her face, crimson with anger, and tried to answer, but though her lips formed the words not a sound came from them. At last, in a voice broken with passion and with words stumbling one over the other, she said, "I— yes—it's so. I—told Mr. Roche not to call the servants. No one asked you to come here. You have no business in this house—looking into things that do not concern you. Mr. Slyke is dead, and every one will believe that he killed himself in spite of anything you can say. Anything that has to be done Mr. Roche can do. It's none of your business, any way."

Standing in front of us with her figure straight and her shoulders thrown back defiantly, she almost shrieked the last words at us. She was so angry that she did not seem to know what she was saying. I wondered why she should be in such a rage. So far as I could see, there was no reason for it. We stood silent and embarrassed. Bartley's eyes never left her face. Under his grave scrutiny she flushed and her eyes dropped.

"Miss Potter," he said suddenly, "you don't want me to believe that you know who killed your brother in law, do you?"

His question seemed the last straw. She turned on him like a fury, and her eyes roved over the desk as if she were looking for something to throw at him. She shrieked, "You say I know who killed him—I—I know? Why, I don't even believe that he was murdered. How dare you say that—how can you stand there and say it to my face?"

Bartley shrugged his shoulders. "I don't say that you know, but if you keep on acting like this whenever you are asked a question someone else will. If it should come out at the inquest, for instance, that you refused to allow us to question the servants, people may not only think you know, but they may go even further. If you don't aid us, Roche can arrest you for obstructing an officer in the performance of his duty."

This was news to her. Anger gave place to fear, and she looked at us helplessly. Bartley realized that, overcome by what she had been through, she was not herself, and added kindly, "I know this death must have shocked you terribly, Miss Potter. I am trying my best to make it easier for you. I did not force myself into the house. Doctor King himself asked me to come this morning. For that matter, Mr. Slyke himself knew that I was to come today to talk with his stepdaughter about that robbery a year ago. What you do not seem to comprehend is that a serious crime has been committed. Your brother in law has been murdered, and the law will demand to know who did it. It will also want to know if you did everything in your power to help us to discover the murderer. No matter what you do, or fail to do, you cannot escape publicity, but you can soften its effects if you will aid us."

She had been nervously moving some books about on the desk. For a moment she said nothing, then she turned and faced Bartley, her eyes searching his, and in the tone of one weary and broken she said, "I will do what I can to help you."

She hesitated and brushed the unkempt hair again and again from her eyes, as if hardly knowing what she was doing.

"It's driving me wild. I am half crazy," she cried suddenly, and taking an uncertain step forward stumbled almost to her knees.

Bartley placed his arm around her and led her to a chair. Then turning to Roche, he asked him to call the servants.

As soon as Roche had gone, Bartley began to examine the room. It had not been cleaned since the night before. A few feet away from him were three card tables, their surfaces littered with playing cards, just as they had been thrown down when the last game was over; so, too, the chairs were in the same position into which they had been pushed when the players rose for the last time. Bartley picked up the cards on the nearest table and counted them. He did the same thing with those on the second table and on the third. At the last table he paused longer than he had at the other two. Finally he took from his pocket the two cards we had found in the tower and motioned to me to join him.

Miss Potter was paying no attention to us. She was lying back in her chair with eyes closed, her whole figure showing the strain that she had been under. As I reached Bartley's side, he asked me to count the cards on the table. I did so and found the pack was two cards short. As

I finished, he handed me the two cards that we had found upstairs saying, "Look at these."

I scanned the two cards he gave me and then those on the table. The pack was an ordinary one, such as is sold for a dollar. Not only the designs on the backs were the same, but the texture of the cardboard as well.

"Do you realize what that shows?" asked Bartley.

"That the cards we found in the tower are from the pack on this table."

"Yes! They may have been dropped up there by the murderer, or they may have been placed there to make us believe that someone in the poker party had committed the crime."

"Why couldn't it have been done," I suggested, "by someone in the party?"

He was thoughtful for a second or two, then slowly shook his head. "Of course, it might have been, but I think that the odds are against it. The finding of the two cards in the tower makes me believe more than ever that the whole thing was a put up job. They were too apparent. This is no ordinary crime, though someone wanted us to think it was a common place suicide. The criminal was afraid, however, that we might discover it to be murder and prepared for that emergency."

"How do you make that out?" I asked, astonished.

"An ordinary criminal"—Bartley spoke so softly that Miss Potter could not hear—"would never have taken all the trouble involved in undressing Slyke and placing him in bed. That was intended to give the idea of suicide; but, as the murderer knew there was a chance of someone suspecting that it was murder, he took the cards from the table and placed them where we could find them. He knew that the finding of cards in the tower would throw suspicion upon everyone present at the game. It is to me only an additional link in evidence that proves it was not suicide."

He added that the crime was not the work of an ordinary criminal, but of a person of great intelligence, one who had not only known how to make it appear to be suicide but had cleverly manufactured other evidence in case it should be discovered to be murder. Such a crime appealed to Bartley, for it involved a problem seemingly without a clue or apparent solution. Our trip to solve a simply burglary had led us into one of the most complex murder mysteries of our experience.

Roche returned, bringing with him the butler, three women and a boy. It had been my experience in other cases that servants become badly frightened when the police question them about a crime, and these women were no exception. They picked nervously at their aprons and looked like a group of children lined up before their teacher, not knowing for what offence they were being called to account. None of them could give us any information of value. The cook, a stout Irish woman of fifty or more, had gone to bed about ten and had slept soundly until morning. She had not even known that Slyke was dead until the butler had told her. The two chambermaids, who slept together in a room off the cook's, had also gone to bed at the same hour and had heard nothing. They, too, said that the first they had known of Slyke's death was when the butler came into the kitchen. It was easy to see that they were telling the truth, and Bartley soon dismissed them.

After they had gone, Bartley turned to the boy who, from the excited way he was wriggling, evidently wanted to say something. It came out with an eagerness that was almost laughable.

"I heard a gun last night," he cried.

"You did?" asked Bartley, startled for a second.

The boy nodded, eagerly.

"Yes, sir. Last night, sir."

Bartley placed his head on the boy's shoulder. "Where were you when you heard the shot? What time was it?"

"Well, sir," the boy began, "you see I work out in the garage, wash the cars and such things. I sleep over it and eat in the kitchen. Last night, you know, we had the big car out to take some of the gentlemen home that were at the card party. When the chauffeur got back I washed the car."

The chauffeur? We stared inquiringly at each other, and Bartley said sharply to Roche, "Where is he?"

Roche looked confused and shamefaced, then hurried from the room, and Bartley resumed his examination of the boy.

"You said you were washing the car. What then?"

"Yes, sir. I was washing the car. It was after twelve o'clock and it took some time. Then I smoked a cigar a man had given me and went to bed. Just after I crawled in, about half past one, I guess, I heard a shot. Not very loud, but it was a shot, all right."

"Where did it seem to come from?" Bartley asked.

The boy scratched his head for a moment and looked a bit foolish as he replied, "It's funny, but it seemed to be up in the air near the house."

Bartley threw me a quick glance. I knew what was in his mind. This fitted in with his theory that Slyke had been killed on the balcony of the tower. If that theory was right and the shot that the boy had heard was the one that had killed Slyke, he would naturally think that the sound came from the air. I wondered if the boy could tell us anything else of value.

"Did you get out of bed to see if you could discover where the shot came from?"

"No, sir, I did not; but, if I had known that Mr. Slyke had killed himself, you bet your life I would."

From his answer I judged that the servants did not yet know that their master had been murdered. At least, this boy did not know. He had told us all he knew about the crime, and was soon sent from the room. Only Miss Potter and the butler now remained to be examined.

Roche returned, looking more shamefaced than ever. "I'm sorry, Mr. Bartley, but I can't find him. No one has seen the chauffeur, and he doesn't seem to be anywhere about the place."

Bartley accepted his statement with a shrug of disappointment, and turned his attention to the butler.

He was a man of about fifty five, tall, with a rather thin face of the unemotional kind common to butlers. We found he had been with Slyke for many years, remaining in his position more because there was so little work to do than from any great love of the man for whom he worked. Though he refused to meet Bartley's eyes, he did not seem to be in the least nervous. What had taken place that night he evidently accepted as something he could not help and need not worry over.

Bartley asked him first about the men that were at the card party. To my surprise the butler said he was unable to give the names of all the men, though he knew most of them. He said that such card parties took place every two or three weeks, and that about the same men came to all of them. The stakes were never very high, and no one man, so far as he knew, had ever lost or, for that matter, won very much. His duties the evening before had been simply to bring in cigars and fresh glasses. He may have been in the room some ten times in all. From what he said, I judged that no one in the group had killed Slyke to recover money that he had lost, for Slyke was one of those who seldom won.

Bartley took down in a little red notebook the names of such men as he could remember. Then he asked suddenly, "And what was the name of the man that stayed after the others left?"

The question seemed to surprise the butler, but he answered, "Mr. Lawrence, sir, the lawyer from Saratoga. Mr. Slyke asked him himself to remain after the others had gone. He went with him up to Mr. Slyke's room. and stayed there a few moments. I myself waited here in a chair to let him out and lock up. I did not have to wait long; not more than ten minutes or so."

Bartley glanced at the stairs.

"Did Mr. Slyke come down with Mr. Lawrence?" he asked.

"No sir. I never saw Mr. Slyke again." He paused, then added slowly, "That is, alive."

"And you did not hear the revolver shot, the one the boy heard?"

"No, sir, I did not."

Bartley took several turns around the room, pausing to glance out of the window; then he came back to the desk and said, "And after you locked up, what did you do?"

"Went to my room. Mr. Slyke had told me not to bother to straighten up this room until morning."

He paused, as if waiting for Bartley to ask him another question. I felt that he was carefully choosing his words and was not giving any more information than he had to. I wondered what it was that he was holding back. Bartley's next question and the answer that it brought proved that I was right.

"Did you see or hear anything last night out of the way?"

The butler was so long in answering that the question had to be asked a second time. That he had heard it the first time I knew, for his eyes flashed as he raised them for a second to Bartley's face. Even after Bartley had repeated his question a second time, he did not answer at once.

We were getting impatient before he said, "I heard nothing suspicious, but I saw—"

He paused, and Bartley urged, "You saw what!"

The butler glanced from Bartley to the woman in the chair. Miss Potter was looking at him with a curious expression on her face, one not of fear but of wonder, as if she were curious to know what his statement meant.

After glancing at her, he turned to Bartley and said apologetically, "Why, sir, I don't know if what I saw was anything out of the way. I would not have thought of it again if Mr. Slyke had not been found dead. When I got to bed, I began to wonder if I had locked the windows. We were rather fussy about them since the robbery. The more

I thought of it the less sure I was; so I got up and was starting to go down into the living room when I saw Miss Ruth, dressed in a long coat, going into her room."

Miss Potter gasped and asked the butler in great astonishment, "But, Robert, how can you say that! You know Miss Ruth was not at home last evening. She spent the night at Saratoga. She has not returned yet."

The butler hesitated and half swallowed, as if he did not wish to contradict his mistress.

"I know, madam, but all the same I saw her. I knew that she was going to be away all night, that was why I was so startled when I saw her going into her bedroom."

Her voice rang out high and clear in the still room, "But, Robert, Miss Ruth was not here last night."

For a second no one spoke. Bartley's eyes went from the butler to the woman and back again. We all wondered what his next question would be, but we never found out. Suddenly, from above us, a girlish voice called, "Who is talking about me?"

Astonished, we all turned and looked in the direction from which the voice had come. On the top step of the stairway a young girl of nineteen years stood looking down at us.

For several seconds Miss Potter seemed unable to believe her eyes, then she half gasped, "Why, Ruth– "

The girl, surprised at the effect her simple question had made, clutched her blue silk dressing gown closer about her and started down the stairs. It was plain that she had just gotten out of bed and had not yet had time to dress. Her eyes went from one person to another questioningly. "Who were we, and what were we doing here?

As she came slowly down the steps we watched her in silence. She was a handsome girl with beautiful red hair and the creamy white skin that goes with it. When she reached her aunt's side, Miss Potter was still too astonished to speak and the girl gave Roche an appealing look. She was beginning to realize that something was wrong. But Roche also was too confused to answer her, and she turned back to her aunt.

"Have the burglars been here again?" she asked.

Not trusting herself to speak, Miss Potter shook her head. The girl knew nothing of the tragedy that had taken place, evidently, or she would not have been so carefree. She waited, and as her aunt did not seem able to tell her what had happened she turned again to Roche. He was still so embarrassed that he shifted from one foot to the other and looked appealingly at Bartley, but Bartley gave him no aid; and after swallowing hard for a moment or two the chief stammered out, "Why, Miss Ruth, you see, we—that is—well, Mr. Slyke has been killed."

The laughing look in her eyes faded and one of surprise, blended with horror, took its place. For a second, that to me seemed an hour, she waited, steadying herself by her hand on the table. Then she asked slowly, almost spelling out each word, "Dead—dead—why— how?"

Again a silence. No one wanted to tell her what had taken place. Her eyes sought each one of us in turn and then rested on Bartley, as if she recognized that he was in charge. A glance passed between the two, then he told her what we had found. The girl could scarcely believe him; and, in fact, when he had finished his story she turned to her aunt as if to ask for confirmation. Miss Potter gave it by a nod.

Though the girl had been startled, I noticed that she was not overwhelmed with grief. Neither had the older woman been. In fact we had yet to hear any word of regret that Slyke was dead. That the girl's astonishment at Bartley's story had been genuine there was no doubt; still the butler's assertion that he had seen her go into her room when she was supposed to have been away from the house had to be explained. Her unexpected presence here this morning seemed to add color to his statement. A glance at her dressing gown with her nightdress peeping beneath it showed that she had just come from her bed. Yet her aunt's surprise at her appearance had also seemed genuine.

"Your aunt told us," Bartley said to her, "that you were away, spending the night with a friend; but the butler says he saw you early this morning going into your own room."

The girl flushed, as if she realized the gravity of her position, and sank into a chair before she answered, "I did intend to spend the night with a friend in Saratoga. On our way home from a dance at the lake our machine lost a tire and it took so long to replace it that, as we were near the house, I decided to come home. Not wishing to go through the woods alone at that hour, I got Uncle Richard to come with me."

Seeing that we were puzzled by the mention of her uncle, she explained that he was really a cousin of her stepfather whom she called uncle. He was a retired clergyman who, during the summer, lived on the estate in a little cottage facing the main road near the entrance to the driveway to the house. When asked if her uncle had come into the house with her she replied that he had not; that he had only waited long enough for her to unlock the front door. She herself had gone directly to her own room, passing the door of her stepfather's room, which had been closed. She had seen no one and heard nothing. She had slept until our voices had awakened her.

Her story, of course, would have to be checked up, but her actions were frank and her manner seemed truthful. She could evidently throw no light on our problem. She waited quietly for Bartley's next question, which, when it came, was a surprise even to me.

"Did you see the dog when you came in?"

"Oh, yes! He came to the door and walked to the foot of the stairs with me."

Bartley turned to the butler and asked, "Was the dog in this room when you came down this morning?"

"Yes, sir. He always sleeps here."

There was a long silence after this, broken at last by the girl asking if she might return to her room. Bartley smiled and assented. I could see that he was not satisfied at the way things had gone. His lips were shut tight and his eyes wandered restlessly around the room. He glanced moodily down at the woman in the chair, who had recovered her composure to some extent, and was now watching with keen eyes everything that was going on.

After a while, Bartley turned to the butler "Did you see anyone near the door of Mr. Slyke's room while we were in there?"

"Why, I don't know, sir. I did see the chauffeur coming down the stairs. But I don't know if he had been up to the room."

"If you can find him, send him to me at once," Bartley commanded.

The butler took this order as a dismissal and left the room. Bartley turned to Miss Potter and asked her if she had returned to Slyke's room after she left us there. She shook her head. There was again a long silence. At length Bartley broke it by telling her that she need not remain any longer. She rose to her feet and started toward the stairway. Half way across the floor she paused, and said in a voice that hesitated more than once, "You asked me, Mr. Bartley, if, when I found Mr. Slyke was dead, I touched the bed clothes."

Bartley turned quickly. The tone of his voice as he answered her question showed that he knew something important was coming.

"Yes, I did."

With her hands playing nervously with a fold of her dress and her eyes on the floor, she continued slowly, "I did not touch the bed clothes, but—I—I- "

"Yes," encouraged Bartley. "You did what?"

She seemed to find it difficult to answer. "When—I went in that room—and found him dead"—her voice was very low—"he looked— I mean, his eyes so frightened me that I—" she paused again—"I closed them."

For a while we looked at her, too surprised to speak. Bartley's brows knit and a curious look came into his face.

All at once I realized the full meaning of her words. If she had closed Slyke's eyes, then it would be hard for Bartley to prove that he had been murdered. He had claimed that, if Slyke had committed suicide, his eyes would have been open. He had gone even further and said it was the murderer who had closed his eyes, thinking that was the way they should look in death. But now Miss Potter had told us that it was she who had closed them. Slyke might, after all, have killed himself! Would Bartley still be able to prove that he had been murdered?

Once more Miss Potter lapsed into her old sullen mood and refused to add anything further. Bartley plied her with questions, but in the end she had added nothing to her first statement that Slyke's staring eyes had frightened her and she had closed them. She insisted, however, that she had not touched the bed clothes, that they had been close around his neck and up over his chin when she had found him.

When we were alone, Roche turned to Bartley and said, "There goes your theory of murder. You can't prove now that he did not kill himself."

Bartley smiled, shrugged his shoulders, and replied, "I am just as sure as ever that he was murdered. In fact, the thing that has been bothering me is not that his eyes were closed when they should have been open—whether he was murdered or killed himself they should be the same—but the position of the bed clothes, and the way his arms were placed at his side, and the manner in which his hand held the gun, as well as a few other things which I have not mentioned. All these prove to me that someone killed him."

"Maybe you are right. But you won't get many people to accept your theory," was Roche's reply.

Bartley made no answer, and Roche continued, "Where are we going to get off in this thing, Mr. Bartley.

What are we going to do? If you are right and he was murdered—(and I guess you are)—there is not even a clue as to who did it, nor why."

Roche was right. We were all at sea. We knew little more about the crime than when we had come into the house early in the morning. True, we knew now that he had been killed on the balcony of the tower and not in his room. But why anyone should go to all the trouble of carrying the body down two flights of stairs and place it in bed I could not see. There was, of course, the remote chance that Bartley was wrong and Slyke had killed himself. If so, why had he done it; or, for that matter, indeed, why had he been murdered? It seemed to me that there were a great many questions that needed answering, and so far we could find the answer to none of them.

Bartley had been listening to Roche with the air of a man whose thoughts were far away. When he paused, he did not reply at once.

"Roche," he said at length, "I feel much about this affair as you do, with the exception that I am sure it was murder, not suicide. It's one of the most mysterious crimes I have ever heard of. We are up in the air. We know of no reason either for Slyke's having been murdered or for his having killed himself. There is a great deal yet to do. You had better get a couple of your men up here as quickly as possible and search the house."

Roche went out to telephone for his men and Bartley walked over to the window. I followed him and we stood looking out at the view. It was about noon, and the dew had gone from the grass and from the roses that covered the side of the house and almost nodded in our faces. Several feet away were other rose bushes that made blotches of flame against the green background of the lawn. I looked at them with interest, for I remembered that it was on one of these that the burglar was claimed to have torn his trousers.

While I was wondering on which one of them the cloth had been found, Bartley made one of his usual unexpected remarks.

"Do you know, Pelt, there is nothing more beautiful than roses in June."

I glanced at him, surprised. He laughed, then becoming serious placed his hand on my shoulder. "Pelt, you have a good deal of work to do today. I want you to find out all you can about the men who were at the poker game. Then you must see that man Lawrence and get his story. Find out why he stayed behind the others. If you have any time left, you had better look up in the files of the local newspaper the burglary of last year."

"You don't think that had anything to do with the murder, do you?" I asked in wonder.

He gave me one of those smiles of his that tell nothing, and drawled out, "I am not saying, but you know we came up here on a burglary case, not a murder mystery."

He did not give me time to wonder what his reply meant, but continued, "Better go to Currie's and get the car, and–"

He might have added more, had not the butler entered. Bartley paused, and taking his note book from his pocket tore out a page and gave it to me. "Here are the names of the men you are to see."

As I was leaving the room he waved his hand and called after me with a smile, "Good luck! See you tonight."

V. In Which I Hear More About The Burglary

CURRIE was sitting on the piazza when I reached the house. He got up hurriedly and advanced to me.

"Where in the devil is John?" he asked.

He apparently knew that we had called over to Slyke's, but he did not know the reason. I answered, "He is over at Slyke's; Slyke was murdered last night."

His large red face grew purple. If it had not been for the seriousness of the news, I would have laughed at the way his jaw dropped and his large eyes stared at me.

"Murdered?" he gasped. "My God, who— who did it?"

I told him all I knew. He listened with intense interest and growing horror. When I ended by saying that Bartley would be back to dinner, he shrugged his shoulders.

"There goes my visit with John. I have been after him for a long time to come up here; and when he does, he finds a murder right on my doorstep." He paused, then added, "I wonder who killed Slyke. I never liked him very much, but I know of no reason for his being murdered."

He wanted me to wait for luncheon, but I refused. Then he suggested that he should go into Saratoga with me, but I again refused his offer. I knew that I should need all the time I could have to carry out Bartley's instructions. I went to the garage and backed out his runabout, and started for town. It was not a long ride, perhaps four miles, and within a few minutes I was driving down the main street, which was bordered by many fine homes, set back on green lawns, and great hotels, now mostly closed, as the racing season was still four weeks away.

In front of the post office I stopped the car and got out. I knew that if the postmaster would give me the addresses of the men who had been at the card party, it would save me a lot of time. Upon explaining my errand, he gave me the desired information. Most of the men were business men from a distance who had summer homes in or around the town, though a few lived the entire year around in Saratoga. One of the first names on the list was that of the editor of the local newspaper, and it suggested an idea to me.

Arriving at the newspaper office, I found the man I sought just going out to luncheon. He was one of those well set up men whose appearance labels him as "a good sport". The red tie, even, was not lacking to his gray suit. When I told him whom I represented, he looked rather anxious as if he were not sure just which one of his secret sins was coming home to roost. When he learned, however, that I had come to ask him some questions about Slyke, he gave a relieved little laugh and invited me to lunch with him.

We went to his club, and in a small dining room found a table to ourselves. Although there were but two other men in the room, I did not tell him what I wanted until we had finished eating; and even then I was very careful of what I told him, although he was a newspaper man and would have most of the facts of the crime in his possession within a few hours.

When I mentioned the list of names, he gave me a keen look, understanding at once what I wanted. Leaning back in his chair, he told me all that he knew. A few men, mostly old friends, met every week or so to play poker. They went to Slyke's usually because, as he put it, "Slyke had more booze than the rest of us." The games were friendly affairs and the stakes low. When I asked him if Mr. Lawrence stayed after the others had gone home, he replied that he had and that he thought Slyke himself had asked him to remain, though he did not know for what reason. As Lawrence had his own car, none of them had waited for him.

I asked him if Slyke had seemed nervous or acted at all strangely that evening. He shook his head. On the contrary, he said, he had seemed more cheerful than usual. He told me that Slyke was always more or less nervous and lost his temper quickly, and was not over-well liked by any of the others. Suddenly it occurred to him that what he had said might place Lawrence in an awkward position.

"Jim Lawrence," he said, "could have had nothing to do with Slyke's death. Lawrence is so darned nervous himself that he would never have dared to fire a gun. It's too bad he stayed behind last night."

Seeing that I was surprised that he knew of the crime, he told me that Doctor King had sent the newspaper word of it, saying that it was a toss up as to whether Slyke had been murdered or had killed himself. I informed him that no one had thought of accusing Lawrence of killing Slyke; but I did not add that, so far as we knew, Lawrence was the last person to see him alive.

As I wanted to interview Lawrence next, the editor accompanied me in the car to point out the building where Lawrence had his office. Here he left me, saying that if I would call at his office in about an hour, he would have the back files of the newspaper I wanted ready for me.

Lawrence's office was on the second floor of a brick building, and his door bore the sign "Law Office." Pushing it open, I entered an outer office. There I found a stenographer idling away her time. She told me Mr. Lawrence was in his private office and that I could enter unannounced. In response to my knock, a voice bade me "Come in."

At a desk, reading a newspaper, was a man of about forty five, with a very thin, nervous face. He threw down the paper and eyed me questioningly. When I told him that Slyke was dead and that I had come to learn about his interview with him, he moved uneasily in his chair; but when I added that we believed that Slyke had been murdered, and that as far as we knew he was the last person to see him alive, he was absolutely unnerved. I could see that, until I mentioned the word murder, he had thought that Slyke had committed suicide. For a second I wondered if, after all, he had not had something to do with the crime. But the longer I looked at him, the more I realized that he was only one of those extremely nervous individualities that are upset by any unfavorable news.

Taking a chair by his side, I said, "You were the last person, so far as we can discover, to see Mr. Slyke alive. We know that you stayed for a few moments only, and that he himself asked that you remain. As you were the last one to see him alive, we are much interested in what you can tell us of how he acted. Did he seem nervous or upset?"

My question did not make the man by my side any easier. He was beginning to realize that, by staying after the others had left, he had become involved in the case. He answered quickly, in a high pitched voice that broke several times, "I did stay; but the other men will tell you that I was going home with them until Slyke asked me to wait a moment. I had no idea beforehand what he wanted. I wish to God I had gone with the rest. Some damned fool will say I killed him."

It was just what some people would say, when it became public that the butler had not heard Slyke's voice again after Lawrence's departure. But for myself, I could not connect guilt with the thin, nervous figure beside me.

"It is, of course, unfortunate that you were the last person, so far as we know, to see Slyke alive. People will talk, but if your own conscience is clear, you shouldn't worry," I encouraged him.

"Yes," he agreed, nodding earnestly, "that's true. I was with him only ten minutes. When I left, the butler opened the front door for me. Slyke didn't leave his room as he said I knew my way out."

"What did he want to see you about?" I asked.

Lawrence flushed, then half grinned, as he answered, "He asked me if I wanted to buy some Scotch whiskey."

"Buy some whiskey?" I repeated in astonishment.

"Yes, it seems foolish, doesn't it? But that's what he wanted to see me about. He said he had lots more than he needed, and that he could let me have five cases."

I said nothing, trying to digest this astonishing information.

He continued, "You know the stuff's getting hard to pick up, so, of course, I said I would take it."

I had been wondering what it was that Slyke wanted to see Lawrence about, and had even made several guesses; but never in my wildest imagination had I supposed that it was about whiskey. I could understand why Lawrence should want to buy it, for good whiskey is hard to get; but why Slyke, presumed to be a rich man, should want to sell five cases was beyond my comprehension.

He saw my surprise and said, "It does seem strange. I was surprised myself. I had heard that he had a lot of booze; but we were not the closest of friends, and nowadays a man lets his liquor go only to his pals. The man who will let you have five cases of whiskey is a pretty good friend."

I smiled at his answer. He was right. People with imported liquor were not giving it away. And what was more, few men of Slyke's position were selling their private stock.

"He told me," Lawrence continued, "that he had a great deal more than he could use, and that he would sell me some for one hundred dollars a case. That's pretty cheap for imported stuff."

The price was low, as he said. A case of imported whiskey brought as high as two hundred dollars. Again I expressed my surprise, and Lawrence agreed with me. His tone was sad as he added that now he doubted if he would ever get it.

"And then you left him?" I asked.

"Yes. He told me he was not going to bed yet. Said someone was coming in about half-past one."

Here was a new piece of evidence. Slyke, then, had not gone to bed after Lawrence left, but had waited up for some other visitor. It was curious, to say the least. One o'clock in the morning is not a usual hour for receiving callers.

"Have you any idea who it was?"

"No," he said, shaking his head, "I haven't the least idea. As I was starting to go he said, 'Stay awhile. I am expecting a man about two and have to wait up for him.' That's all I know about it."

It was not much of a clue, still it was better than nothing. It did establish the fact that there had been someone else with Slyke that night. That is, if he were telling the truth. The burning question in my mind was, who was that second person? Was he the one who had killed Slyke? The odds seemed to favor it. Lawrence had little further information to give me. He said that Slyke had not been especially, nervous, nor had he acted like a man afraid of anything. He added that he had no enemies in the little group that had been playing poker with him.

I rose to go, but paused at a new thought.

"Oh, Mr. Lawrence, did Slyke give you a drink?"

He had accompanied me to the door, and paused, one hand on the knob. "Yes, he did, up in the room over his sleeping room. He got out a bottle and two glasses and we had a drink."

"You did not see three glasses, did you?"

"No," he answered, surprised at my question. 'No, only two."

Thanking him, I said good by and left.

When I returned to the newspaper office, I found the files of the past year awaiting me. It was a typical country paper, and the burglary that had taken place at Slyke's was naturally, for it, a big piece of news. For many days the story of the various happenings had been spilled all over the front page. Then for a while there was nothing. But when the trial began, the front page was again filled with full accounts of the testimony. It took me several hours to read it all, and when I had finished I had a fairly good idea of all that had taken place. The story that Rogers told us in Bartley's library, and the account of the crime in the paper were substantially the same. There were, however, one or two slight differences that seemed to me important. I had understood Rogers to say that the step daughter, Ruth, had positively identified the men now in prison; but nowhere in the newspaper was it stated that this had been the case. What she had actually said was, "I think one of them is the man I saw in the room." There had been no positive identification of the men by her, or by anyone else, for that matter. Slyke himself had testified that he did not know whether they were the men or not.

Three things had convicted them. First, the piece of paper found in the room where the burglary had taken place, and which fitted into a torn corner of a newspaper discovered later in the coat of one of the men; second, the piece of cloth said to have been found on a rose bush beneath the window of the room entered, and which fitted the torn place in a pair of trousers belonging to one of the men—there was some doubt as to whether the trousers had been torn at the time the man was arrested—and last of all, the footprints under the window. Thus their conviction rested on a piece of torn newspaper and a hole in a man's trousers—rather feeble evidence, it seemed to me. Moreover, the police had not discovered any of it until some days after the crime. The more I thought of it, the more I agreed with Bartley that the case was remarkably like that old burglary case in England.

Leaving the newspaper office, I called on some of the other men who had been at the card party. They all agreed that it was Slyke who had suggested Lawrence's staying, and laughed at the idea that he knew anything about his death. One of them told me that, several weeks before, he had bought three cases of whiskey from Slyke. I could not understand why a man of Slyke's position should wish to sell whiskey to his friends. To this man also he had given the excuse that he had more than he needed for his own use.

As I passed the court house on my way home, I noticed the words "District Attorney's Office" on a window, and it occurred to me that stored away somewhere in there would be the exhibits in the burglary case. I entered and asked to see the torn piece of paper and the bit of cloth. The only person in the room was a boy of eighteen, who went into a back room and returned with a box under his arm. Opening it, he shook out on the desk before me a newspaper, saying, "This is the paper they found in the man's pocket. You can see the torn edge."

He pointed to the front sheet of the newspaper, one corner of which had been torn away. Lifting another piece of paper from the box, this time a small one, he fitted it into the torn corner. I glanced at the heading of the paper. It was a copy of the "Boston Evening Times," and the date was that of the day before the burglary. The piece of cloth was next shown me. After examining it I thanked the boy, and returned to the car.

I felt that I had accomplished very little by my afternoon's work. The only new evidence was Lawrence's statement that Slyke had been expecting someone after he left. I wished that he had accepted Slyke's invitation to remain until this other person came. With the exception of this and Slyke's having offered to sell whiskey to two different men, a fact that could have no bearing on the murder, I had found out nothing.

In my hurry to get back for dinner, I took the wrong road and landed at Saratoga Lake, four miles beyond the town. Turning the car, I retraced my way, but it was long after six before I drove up to the house. The butler met me at the door with the message that they were awaiting dinner for me, and that I must hurry.

After a rapid toilet, I descended to find Bartley talking with Mrs. Currie, who had returned during the afternoon. Like her husband, she was an old friend of his, having lived next door to him when a child. She was a little younger than her husband, with dark hair and eyes that were always smiling. I was introduced and we went in to dinner at once.

It was served in the sun parlor so that we might enjoy, as we ate, the view of the fields and woods and of the far distant hazy mountains. Mrs. Currie told us that we were not to be treated as guests but as members of the family, and joked Bartley on the long time it had taken him to come to visit them. They spoke of old playmates, and then the conversation wandered to new books. Currie tried several times to mention his farm, but each time his wife held up a warning finger.

When the dessert was over and we were drinking our wine and smoking comfortably, Bartley leaned back in his chair with such a deep sigh of contentment that Currie laughed.

"Better than murders, eh, John?"

Bartley joined in the laugh. "Anything is."

"I have often wondered," Mrs. Currie said thoughtfully, "what causes people to commit murder. They always get found out."

"Not always, Laura," answered Bartley. "I know it's the opinion of most people that a person who commits murder is discovered in the long run, but that is not true. I should say that about eighty per cent of the murders are never solved. There are hundreds of deaths every year that are actually murders, but the police never hear of them. You ask why people kill. As a rule, it is done in rage or in a sudden passion of some kind. Such, crimes are easy to solve. It is the small percentage that are planned that are difficult. You see, we first look for the motive of a crime, and if we can find that we can usually solve it."

Currie, who had been listening carefully, broke in with, "I presume you will solve this Slyke affair quickly."

Bartley was silent, watching the smoke of his cigar curl toward the ceiling. His face was expressionless when he replied, "Oh, I can't tell, Bob. I have not found anything of importance yet."

I glanced at him in surprise. It seemed impossible that he could have spent a whole day at Slyke's and not have discovered something of value.

Mrs. Currie turned to her husband. "Bob, what are you men going to do this evening? You know this is the night of my musicale."

Currie gave such a groan that we all laughed. "There is a long haired tenor coming here tonight, and a crowd of women who will roll their eyes at him and lie like the devil, murmuring 'How beautiful!' It's no place for us. We'll go to Saratoga and come back when it is all over."

Mrs. Currie placed her hand reprovingly over her husband's mouth. He rolled his eyes at us and winked, and even his wife laughed as she said, "It's not as bad as Bob says, John, but you men would not enjoy it."

Before we started Currie said he had to give some orders to his men, and Bartley and I went to our rooms. I gave him a brief outline of what I had discovered in Saratoga. He did not ask any questions until I mentioned that the newspaper from which the corner had been torn, was a copy of the "*Boston Evening Times*," then he asked the date of the issue. When I told him it was that of the day before the robbery, he took his cigar from his mouth, grinned, and threw out his hands in an expressive gesture.

"That's enough to prove those men had nothing to do with the burglary. You know the '*Times*' is an evening paper, and is not sold on the newsstands far from Boston—not up here, at any rate. If a copy of the paper had been mailed here, as it would have to be, it could not have reached Saratoga until hours after the robbery had taken place. Such being the case, the men that broke into the house could not have had it with them, nor could the police, have found a piece torn from it in the room the next morning."

I saw his point and was eager to learn what he thought of the other things I had discovered. Above all, I wanted to know what his opinion would be of Lawrence's statement that Slyke was expecting someone to call after he left. To my surprise he was much more interested in the fact of Slyke's having offered the whiskey for sale. A keen look came into his eyes and he allowed his cigar to go out, but made no comment. I had expected, when I had finished with my story, that he would tell me what he had discovered after I left him at Slyke's. But as he did nothing of the sort, I finally found courage to inquire. He had risen to his feet, and, going to the window, glanced out, then returned to my side.

"Well, Pelt," he said with a quizzical smile, "there are two things that I want very much to discover."

"Two?" I questioned.

He seated himself, filled his pipe, lighted it, and when it was drawing to suit him, settled his head back against the chair.

"Yes, two," he said, with a little smile playing around his lips. "The first thing I would like to know is, what has become of Slyke's chauffeur?"

Seeing I did not understand, he went on, "You know we sent for him but they could not find him. Up to the time I left the house they were still looking for him. Not only that, but the chauffeur and Slyke had a quarrel yesterday afternoon."

"A quarrel?"

"Yes. No one was near enough to hear all that was said, but the cook heard the chauffeur say, 'You don't dare to do it,' and Slyke reply, 'I should have done it before.' The butler, you remember, told us that while we were in the tower he saw the chauffeur on the steps leading to the second story. The chap has disappeared, no one knows where. The police are looking for him and may get him. I hope so. There are a few things I should like to ask him."

"Maybe it was he who took the revolver," I suggested.

Bartley agreed. As he did not continue, I asked him what were the other things that he wanted to know.

"Has it occurred to you that it is a strange thing that a man like Slyke should spend most of his time up here? For the past two years he has lived here almost entirely. His office in New York is closed, and he is rumored to have lost money. Why did he stay here all the year round?"

I had not known that Slyke was making Circle Lake his home. It was beautiful in summer, but in the winter it must be very cold. It did seem strange that a man like Slyke should leave New York and make a place like this his home.

Bartley suddenly changed the subject. "Miss Potter cleared up one thing for us, today. I knew that, if the murderer was shrewd enough to go to the trouble of placing Slyke in bed, he knew enough to know how the eyes should look. Their being closed puzzled me. I wondered how he had made such a mistake. But when Miss Potter told us it was she who had closed them, I knew that I had not been mistaken. Whoever killed Slyke knew what he was doing. There was only one chance in a thousand that he would not get it across."

"Only he did not know you were coming."

He laughed. "Well, let's be modest, Pelt. Let's say that he expected to be able to fool the average person. Even doctor King believes yet that it may be suicide. He is wrong. It's murder, all right, but the motive I still have to discover."

"It was well planned," I suggested.

"It was not planned at all. It was a sudden impulse, a quarrel. I don't believe that, when the murderer went into that tower room to see Slyke, he had the least idea of killing him."

"But think of the pains he took. It must have been planned."

"No," he replied, "the planning was done afterward."

"After he was killed?"

"Yes. Look at the facts, Pelt. Slyke was killed on the balcony of a tower, fifty feet above the ground. A man who planned a murder would not pick out such a place. It was the last place in the house he would have chosen. Just suppose that someone had heard the shot and investigated. The murderer would have been trapped with the dead body of his victim. To escape he had to go down two flights of stairs and through the big room. Let us say that Slyke invited the man to go up on the balcony—for what we cannot say—and then they quarreled and the person killed him on the impulse of the moment. The next thing to do was to get rid of the body. Finding the coast clear, he took it into the next room and undressed it, and carried it down to the bedroom and placed it in bed. He knew how a body should look after suicide and that a gun could be placed in its hand."

"He seemed to be pretty sure no one would disturb him at it," I ventured.

Bartley nodded. "Yes, there is no doubt of that. That brings up another astonishing fact. Down in the big room was a young dog that did not like strangers. The murderer, in order to get out of the house, had to go through that room, yet the dog did not bark."

"Then it was someone in the house!" I interrupted.

"The coolness with which the murderer took plenty of time in undressing the body and the fact that he did not seem to be afraid of being found out makes it seem probable. Why didn't the dog bark? Because he knew whoever it was. That makes it seem as if it were someone in the house, or at least as if it were someone that knew both the house and the dog well."

At that moment Currie's voice came loudly from the hall below, "Eh, John, you tin detective, are you ready?"

Bartley chuckled. At the door, with his hand on the knob, he paused. "Of course, Pelt, until we discover the motive we cannot get very far. At present there seems to be none. There is nothing missing and no apparent reason for Slyke's murder. It seems an absurd sort of a crime. That's why I think it was done on impulse, not premeditated." He thought a moment, then added, "I did think I knew the kind of a person that might have committed a crime like this. But–"

"But what?" I asked eagerly.

He opened the door with a little smile on his lips, and it was not until we were half way down stairs that he completed his sentence, "But—I don't know."

VI. The Vault In The Woods

WE found Currie waiting for us in one of his large cars, with his chauffeur. He said that he was going to send the machine home and let us walk back. We did not follow the road that I had taken in the afternoon, but a much longer way that ran between tall trees. There were few cars on the road, and in a very short time we arrived in Saratoga.

We left the car before one of the hotels and followed Bartley to the Public Library. It was a small stone building hidden by ivy and with one large reading room, its sides lined with reference books. Bartley spent several moments glancing through the card catalogue before he crossed to the loan desk, and asked the pretty young librarian for *Griffeth's Mysteries of Crimes*. She returned in a moment with two volumes, bound in red cloth. Bartley opened one to the place where the date when a book is taken out is stamped. There was only one date on the white slip, and Bartley copied it in his notebook. Then, turning to the librarian, he asked her how they had happened to buy the book, and if she knew who it was that had taken it from the library the one time it had gone out.

Looking through her cards, she told them that the book had been a gift, and that the only person that had ever taken it out was James Briffeur. Bartley raised his eyebrows in surprise but did not ask her anything more.

As soon as we were again on the street, he told us that so far as he knew the only account of the Edlingham burglary, other than the one in the rare pamphlet that he owned, had been published in the volumes he had been glancing at. They were written by a former English police magistrate, and were the greatest collection of crime stories ever brought together in one work. Currie, of course, did not understand what he was talking about; and Bartley gave him the details of the English crime, and ended by saying that, from the very first it had been his opinion that whoever had faked the burglary at Slyke's, had read the account of the English crime. Then, with a little rueful smile, he added that the one person who had taken the book from the library was Slyke's chauffeur.

He might have said more had we not reached Currie's club just then. We were introduced to several men; then Currie challenged Bartley to a game of billiards and was thoroughly beaten. After the game was over we sat and talked until about eleven o'clock; then we started home.

As we were leaving the club, we met a young man whom Currie introduced to us as Captain Lowe, commander of the local branch of the state police. He was bronzed like all those who live much in the open, and wore a pin on his coat, showing that he had seen service in France. As he was going in our direction, we fell into step together; and he told us of his work and how the state troopers had reduced crime so much that farmers' wives now had a sense of security, even in the most remote country districts. The greatest trouble they had at present, he told us with a laugh, was with the smuggling of whiskey, not only into Saratoga but even as far as Albany and Troy. Though they knew that a good deal of whiskey was getting through, they could not discover who was running it. At the barracks he bade us good night.

It was rather dark after we left the lights of the town behind, and Currie inquired with a sigh, why in the devil a man who owned four automobiles should have been fool enough to suggest walking home. Bartley tried to cheer him by reminding him that he was getting fat and needed the exercise, but Currie did not seem to appreciate his efforts. It was a fine evening, the air cool and clear with light enough to enable us to see a few feet ahead of us. At first the road ran between fields and by the lawns of the

great estates; then it entered a stretch of woodland, and
we had to walk very slowly because of the darkness.
Every once in a while I heard Currie smother a mild oath
as he stumbled over a stone.

As we passed the driveway that led into the Slyke
grounds, he told us that it ran through nearly a mile of
dense woods before it reached the house. We were about a
thousand feet beyond the entrance when Bartley
suddenly stopped.

"What's that?" he asked in a low voice.

I listened a moment, but the only thing I could hear
was the horn of a distant automobile.

Bartley continued, "I thought I heard a car in the
woods, there on the left."

Currie, who was a few feet in front of us, laughed.
"John," he said, "you're hearing things. No car can be in
those woods. Those are the trees you see from my house,
and they stretch for some miles without a break. Slyke
owns this part of them. You could not have heard a car."

Bartley placed his hand on his friend's shoulder.
"That's what I thought, Bob. But I did hear a motor; of
that I am sure."

He paused, then added suddenly, "Listen! There it is
once more."

This time we all heard the faint sound of a motor
running slowly and with difficulty. There was no doubt of
it, it came from the woods before us. It sounded as if a car
were running a few feet, then stopping, as it would do on
a very bad road when having difficulty in getting
through.

As we all stood listening to the strange sound coming
through the woods, Bartley said, "You say, Currie, that
there is no road there, yet by the sound of it I should say
that was a truck. What do you say to going and finding
out what it means?"

Currie gave an exclamation of disgust. "But it's none
of our business, John."

"Just at the present moment, everything that takes place on Slyke's estate is our business. I want to know what a car is doing in those woods at this time of night."

"Oh, I'm game if the rest of you are," Currie responded.

With a caution from Bartley not to make any noise, we left the road and entered the woods. It was lucky for us that there were not many vines or much underbrush, or we should not have gotten very far. There was no path, and we fell over stumps and broken branches and bumped into trees at almost every step. The further we went from the road the darker it became. Bartley had a pocket torch with him, but he did not want to use it. Once or twice, though, he did flash it for a second so that we could disentangle ourselves from the vines that had wrapped themselves around our feet.

With Bartley in the lead, Currie close behind him, and myself last of all, we pushed on, pausing at times to listen for the sound of the motor. It grew louder and louder, and I knew that we were catching up with it. It was very lucky for us that the truck could not go very fast and had to stop frequently, or it would have gotten away from us.

We had not heard the motor for several moments when a car loomed so suddenly out of the shadowy darkness ahead of us that we almost fell over it. It was a great truck, loaded with small cases. Upon its top, a little darker than the night, we made out the figures of two men, while a third disentangled itself from the gloom in front of the car with a muffled oath, and climbed to the driver's seat. The car started forward with a lunge along a road, if it could be called such, that had been made by felling trees and leaving their stumps still standing. The driver must have been familiar with it, for no one who was not could have driven that truck over it without lights.

"I want to get the number," Bartley whispered, as it lurched ahead.

He crept softly up behind the slowly moving car. He need not have been careful, for the truck was making so much noise that no one on it could have heard him. For the faintest part of a second I saw the flash of his light. The next he was back at our side.

"There is no license plate on the car. There's something wrong there. Come along!"

As the truck, lurching from side to side, was not going faster than three miles an hour, we had no difficulty in keeping up with it. The woods were so dark that there was little chance of our being seen; yet we took the precaution to remain at some distance and keep well in the shadow. We had followed it for perhaps five minutes when it came out suddenly onto a road that Currie said led to Slyke's house. Here it paused, the motor running softly. We crept closer and heard a voice say, "Well, Jim, here's to luck. We will make a run of it."

Just at this moment Currie tripped over a root. He tried to save himself, grabbed at my arm, missed, and went to the ground with a loud crash. As he fell, Bartley jerked me to one side and threw me on my face. The sound of Currie's fall was like a young earthquake, and did not escape those on the truck. As I went down I saw one of the men turn and fire. The next second, gaining speed with every foot, the truck shot down the road.

With the truck gone we no longer needed to hide; we rose and rushed to Currie to see if he were shot. As Bartley's light flashed over him, we discovered that he was sitting up, and swearing to himself. His face was covered with dirt and one eye was beginning to turn black, but he was otherwise unhurt.

"John," he demanded, "what the devil made that tire explode?"

"That was not a tire, Bob. Someone on the truck heard you as you fell and took a shot at you."

"Took a shot at me?" cried Currie, in utter disbelief. 'My God, why?"

Bartley helped him to his feet and brushed the dirt from his clothes before he answered, "It's a darned good thing they missed you. Those men on top of the boxes were there to protect them. I wonder what was in them."

Currie was silent for a moment. Then his slow voice drawled out, "Well, anyway, I can never say after this that I haven't been under fire. But I don't see any war cross coming my way."

Bartley was anxious to learn what that truck was doing in the woods, and why the men on it were so determined that no one should know what they were carrying, that they were willing to fire upon anyone who interfered. He told us that it ought to be an easy matter to find where the truck had come from; as all we had to do was to follow back into the woods the tracks the heavily loaded truck had cut in the soft ground.

The intense blackness of the woods was being slowly dissolved by the rising moon. There was no sound except, once in a while, an automobile passing on the main road. As we followed the tracks with the aid of Bartley's pocket torch, we saw that the wheels had sunk a foot into the sod in places, and that more than one heavily loaded truck had passed this way. Now and then one of us would slip and almost fall, and Bartley would flash his light; but, for the most part, we had to follow the ruts in darkness, feeling for them with our feet.

We followed the road for about half a mile before it ended in a clearing, a quarter of an acre square.

Bartley examined the four sides of the clearing carefully before he came back to us and said, in a voice that sounded strange in the darkness, "The road ends here. I have an idea that this is where they got their load."

Currie had been peering through the darkness as the flashes of Bartley's light shot between the trees. "I have a fool idea, John," he said slowly, "that I know where we are."

"You do?" came the eager response.

"Yes. If I am not mistaken, we are within a hundred yards of the old cemetery that is on Slyke's ground. It must be over a hundred years old, and was founded by the early settlers. Several years ago Slyke showed me the place. We had the devil of a time reaching it, for there was no path to it. All there is left of it is an old vault and half a dozen crumbling tombstones."

I was unable to see Bartley's face, but his voice was eager.

"A vault! What kind?" he asked.

"Why," replied Currie, "just a vault. One of those things dug into the side of a hill where dead bodies are placed. If I am right, there is a small hill only a few yards from here."

Bartley turned and, flashing his light on the ground, moved it slowly back and forth as he advanced. He paused and bent to examine the ground.

"I guess I have it," he called to us. "Here are footprints."

Without giving us time to examine them, he went deeper into the woods, and we followed. Some fifty feet from the clearing, the little path. we were on ended abruptly in a small mound.

"It's your vault, Currie," said Bartley.

His light rested on the massive wooden door of an old fashioned burial vault dug out of the hillside and fastened securely by a large lock. As Bartley examined it, he gave a little whistle. "Well, Currie, that may be an old vault, and an old door, but the lock on it is modern. It has been placed there within a short time. I am going to open it."

Currie expressed a most unfavorable opinion of people who fooled around old burial vaults at midnight. What did Bartley expect to find in it anyway, but a lot of bones? He never had liked graveyards, and in the dark he liked them even less.

Bartley replied with a laugh, "There is nothing in the vault that can harm any of us. I want to know why the truck has been in the woods. The vault is the key to the mystery, and I am going to open it."

With a thin piece of wire and a bit of steel, Bartley picked the lock, then flung the door open and turned his flashlight into the darkness within. I think that Currie and myself both held our breath as the light swept back and forth over the walls and floor. It disclosed nothing more startling than a number of boxes, similar to those we had seen on the truck, piled one on the other against the walls. It was plain enough where the load had been gotten.

Bartley led the way in and closed the door behind us. Once more he swept the vault with his torch, and this time we noticed a lantern on a box and lit it.

The vault was about twenty five feet long and had been dug into the side of the hill, but the sides and roof were of stone. Along the walls were niches for coffins, and these were piled high, and the floor as well, with hundreds of small boxes. The flame of the lantern flickered in a draught and queer shadows danced on the walls, while a musty, earthy smell rose half chokingly. It was not the most pleasant place to be in.

But Bartley did not seem to mind it. He stood in the center of the floor, glancing around the vault with such an amused smile that I knew that something had pleased him particularly. Suddenly he went to the nearest box, ripped off the cover, and drew out a bottle. We crowded around him as he removed the paper and disclosed the label of a well known brand of imported whiskey.

"That's what I expected," Bartley commented. "We know now what was on that truck. Captain Lowe won't have to hunt any longer for the place where they hide the smuggled whiskey."

For a moment Currie said nothing. He picked up the bottle, examined it, then replaced it very carefully in the box, saying in a serious tone, "John, that's a darned good brand of whiskey. In times like these, it does seem a shame to turn it over to the police. I don't suppose that I can swipe three or four cases while your back is turned?"

Bartley laughed as he shook his head. He summed up the situation by saying, "When you think that this stuff will sell for at least twenty five thousand dollars, and remember that it did not cost more than three thousand in Canada, you can see why there is money in this game."

He made a careful search of the vault. The boxes lined the walls to a height of six feet on all sides. A few cigarette stubs on the dirt floor showed that someone had been smoking, but there was nothing to indicate whom he might have been. As he finished his examination, Bartley said, "I guess we may as well go now."

I had taken off my hat when I entered the vault, and placed it on one of the boxes, and now when I looked for it I could not find it. It occurred to me that it must have fallen behind a box; and, taking Bartley's torch, I climbed up on one box and flashed the light into the niche behind the one on which I thought I had laid it. There it lay. As I reached for it my hand came in contact with something hard. I knew, even as my fingers groped for the object, that it was a revolver. Climbing down from the box, I went up to Bartley.

"Look what I found!" I exclaimed.

"Where did you get that?" he asked excitedly as he took it from me.

I told him of my hat falling behind the boxes, and how the revolver had been in the niche back of them. There seemed no reason for his being so excited over the find, but his next words enlightened me.

"That's the gun that was in Slyke's hand this morning. I recognize the worn place on the barrel."

"But how did it get there?" I asked in wonder.

"I don't know," was the reply. "It looks as if the person that threw it back of the boxes, did it to hide it. He may intend to come for it later."

To my surprise, he bent over suddenly and blew out the lantern. In a second the vault was in darkness. Currie started to remonstrate, but a warning whisper from Bartley stopped him.

"Both of you get back of that door at once. There is someone outside. Don't make a move or a sound. I think he is going to come in."

I heard Currie mutter in surprise as we groped our way behind the door. At first I could hear nothing; then on the other side of the wooden door I heard some one stumble and a hand fumble for the lock. What could it mean? If the truck had come back for another load we were in a bad fix indeed. The men who had fired at us before would not hesitate to shoot to kill this time, and when we were missing no one would think to search for us in this vault. In a fight, the odds were heavily against us as Bartley alone was armed.

Currie and myself had been placed by Bartley so that when the door opened we would be hidden by it. He took up his position on the other side, crouching flat against the wall. It was too dark to make out his figure, or even that of Currie at my side. I listened to his. uneasy breathing, and for a second wondered what he was thinking about.

Whoever was opening the door, had no fear of making a noise. He stumbled into the vault, and swung the door shut behind him with a little click. Then a slit of light pierced the darkness and we crouched against the wall, scarcely daring to breath, expecting every moment that he would see us. Just what he had come for I never knew. He played the light rather aimlessly along the walls, then turned it onto the floor. All at once it paused, and I heard an astonished gasp. No wonder, for the light was resting on Bartley's shoes.

The next second he had extinguished it and was making for the door. Almost before he had moved, Bartley had flashed on his own torch and was saying, "Put up your hands. I have you covered."

The light in Bartley's hand had been focussed on the man's body, leaving his face in darkness. As he began to move it upward to his face, the man made a swift, flying dive at Bartley's legs. The attack was so sudden that he was taken unawares, and they fell to the floor together. As Bartley went down, he struck the button of his torch and extinguished it, leaving us in darkness. We could hear the two men thrashing about on the floor, but could not tell who was getting the best of it. I groped for the torch but could not find it. Then I remembered the lantern and searched for that. Relighting it, I held it above my head so that the light fell on the floor. Bartley was sitting on the man that had attacked him, his face and white suit streaked with dirt and a lump reddening over one eye, but he was smiling. He directed me to find his torch, which had rolled half under a box, and relight it. When I had complied, he rose to his feet, and, pulling the man up with him, told me to throw the light on the face of his prisoner.

"Let's have a look at this chap."

We saw a black, scowling face, and cruel, shifty eyes that blinked angrily.

Currie cried, "Why, it's Slyke's chauffeur!"

The man did not deny it, but stood silent and glowering. Remembering what Bartley had told me of the butler having seen him on the stairs while we were in the tower rooms, I wondered if he were the one who had placed the revolver here. When Bartley questioned him as to why he had come to the vault he replied that it was none of his business; and when Bartley suggested that the police might make it their business, he only laughed sneeringly. We were discussing what we should do with him, since there was no charge on which he could be arrested, when we received another shock.

The chauffeur had closed the door of the vault when he entered, but in some way it had become unfastened during the struggle, and now stood wide open, the lighted interior plainly visible to anyone without. We were standing grouped together near the center of the room, our backs to the door, when a voice said, "Up with your hands, the whole four of you. Be quick about it! I have you all covered, and will shoot the first one that moves."

There was but one thing to do, and we all did it. With our hands high in the air, we turned to the doorway to see who the intruder was. He was a tall, heavy set man with a round face, holding a revolver in his right hand.

Who could this second man be? For a second I thought it must be some friend of the chauffeur; but one look at his astonished face told me he knew no more who the man was than we did. Bartley looked puzzled, yet a little smile never left his face. Currie held his hands in the air with the manner of a man bored by the whole thing. I almost smiled to myself as I thought of the varied experiences he was so unwillingly undergoing.

The man stood still for a moment before advancing into the vault. It seemed to me that he was startled at finding four of us there. He came to the center of the vault, and stopped, keeping several feet away from us.

"Starting with the man on the right," he said, "come over here, one by one. I am going to search you. No foolishness, now; I will kill the first man that starts something."

"My, what a pleasant man," I heard Currie mutter.

The first man on the right happened to be Bartley. He stepped forward, his hands high in the air. I wondered if he would submit quietly to being searched. He allowed the left hand of the man to go over his clothing until it reached the revolver in his pocket; then like a flash he grasped the hand holding the gun at his chest, and gave it such a quick jerk that the weapon fell to the floor.

The fight was on. Both Currie and myself started to assist him, but Bartley called to us to watch the chauffeur. I picked up the revolver and covered the man.

It was not a long fight, and Bartley soon had his opponent subdued. As he dragged him to his feet, and began to search him, he stopped with an amused cry. On the man's vest was a little badge.

"Why didn't you tell us you were a detective?" he asked.

The man, his face red with rage, answered, "Why in hell should I?"

Bartley explained who he was, and the detective was delighted at the encounter. After we had given him hack his gun and helped him brush himself off, he seated himself on a box, saying, "I will say you work quick, Mr. Bartley."

We grinned at this. We were much relieved to find that he was a detective, and not one of the gang engaged in running whiskey. He told us that he was in the Revenue Department and had been watching Slyke's house for some time, or I should have said, rather, his chauffeur's. He had given him the slip and he had been searching for him all day. He had encountered him about ten o'clock and had been trailing him ever since. When the chauffeur had come to the vault, he had waited for him outside; then the door had swung open and he had seen a chance to capture what he thought was the gang.

He pointed at the chauffeur and said, "That's the chap, I believe, that killed Slyke."

Up to this time the chauffeur had not said a word. His face turned white with rage, and he cried, "You lie!" and would have taken the detective by the throat if Bartley had not prevented him.

Bartley made no comment on the detective's statement; his expressionless face giving no hint as to his thoughts. I remembered the revolver that had been hidden back of the box, and wondered if, after all, the detective might not be right.

Bartley and the detective, whose name was Black, decided that the best thing to do with the chauffeur was to place him in the hands of the police. When Black learned that the vault was filled with whiskey, he asked Bartley to remain and help him guard it until the police could relieve him; he seemed to fear that the rest of the gang would return. Bartley told me to go to the house and call up Roche, and ask him to come at once with his men, and then to bring back his car.

I reached the main road without meeting anyone, and, breaking into a run, was soon at the house. The musicale was over when I arrived and the front driveway was filled with automobiles. I skirted the house and reached the garage unseen. I telephoned at once to Roche; and he was so much startled at my story that I had great difficulty in making him understand where he was to go, and what he was to do. At last he agreed to come at once.

It took me only a few moments in Bartley's car to reach the woods again; but, when I arrived, I saw two other cars already parked on the roadside, and knew that the police had preceded me.

I found Roche and two of his men in the vault, conferring with Bartley and Black. It had been decided to guard the place until morning, when the whiskey could be removed. The chauffeur was to be taken to the Saratoga jail and locked up.

"Well, Mr. Bartley," Black said, when all this had been arranged, "you have solved in one night something the rest of us, including the state police, have been working on for months."

Bartley insisted that it had been mostly a matter of luck.

We left them and walked to his car in silence. As we climbed in Bartley motioned me to the driver's seat, and he and Currie sat behind me. Currie suddenly gave a chuckle.

"John," he said, "are most of your evenings as uneventful as this one?"

Bartley laughed, but did not answer.

When we reached the house, Mrs. Currie, in full evening dress, came to meet us. At the sight of her husband's black eye, which by this time was very noticeable, and the ruin of Bartley's white suit, she gave a little cry.

"What under heaven have you men been doing?" she asked.

Currie gave me a wink. "Looking for whiskey," he answered.

He went to a nearby table, took something from each pocket and placed them carefully upon it. He then stood looking down at them proudly.

"A little souvenir of the night's work," he remarked, pointing to two bottles of whiskey which he had taken, without our knowing it, from the box that Bartley had opened in the vault.

VII. In Which Bartley Talks Of Many Things

MRS. CURRIE wanted to hear the story of our adventures; and when Bartley recounted what had taken place, I noticed that he expressed no opinion as to what was back of it all. When he had finished, Currie insisted that we try some of the whiskey that he had brought back, and we each had a highball.

It was after one when we reached our rooms, and I had expected that Bartley would want to go to bed at once. I knew how tired I was, and supposed that he must be even more weary. But, after he had gotten into his blue silk pajamas, he dropped into a chair by the window, curled one leg over the arm, lighted his pipe, and turned to me. His face wore a quizzical expression and his eyes smiled.

"Well, what do you think of it all?" he drawled.

That was a hard question to answer. We had been through so much, so many apparently unconnected events, that I scarcely knew what to think. Then, too, I knew very little of what had taken place after I had left him at Slyke's, or what new things he had observed there. The finding of the whiskey and the sudden appearance of the chauffeur, coupled with my discovery of the revolver, seemed to me to still further complicate the problem. What had he come to the vault for? I remembered that the detective had said he thought the chauffeur had killed Slyke. I wondered if this was simply a wild guess, or whether there was something behind it.

Bartley watched me with that little smile on his lips that meant so many things. When I explained that I hardly knew what to think, that events had been too rapid for me, he nodded. For a while we sat silent,

Bartley leaning back in his chair, his eyes closed, and the smoke of his cigar drifting lazily out of the open window into the night. He appeared to be resting, but I knew that his brain was going over the events of the day. The cigar was half smoked before he opened his eyes and sat up.

"Well, Pelt," he said, "it looks as if we were engaged upon as mysterious a case as ever came our way. The more I look it over, the less sure I am of anything. Do you know, I picked up very little after you left the house?"

I had been wondering all day if he would find any clues of value. I knew what a careful search he must have made, and his statement that he picked up very little of importance surprised me.

Bartley watched me for a moment or two before continuing, "It's one of the oddest affairs in many ways that I have ever heard of. I don't believe I ever had a case in which there were so few clues, and those of so little value. The criminal usually leaves some trace behind him; but so far, in this case, there is hardly a thing. We are up against a crime that will require a different procedure from that which we generally use. Instead of working from clues to theory, we must turn it about, and each of us build up a theory, and then see if the clues will fit it." He paused, and added, "So far, we have little enough to go on."

He took his pipe from his mouth and carefully refilled it. Then he told me in greater detail of his day's work. They had been unable to find the chauffeur either at the garage or anywhere else around the estate. No one had seen him since the butler saw him on the stairs early in the morning. The cook had later volunteered the information that Mr. Slyke and he had quarreled over something. What it was she did not know; she had only heard the few words he had repeated to me. The house had been searched from top to bottom, but without result. So far as he could tell, nothing had been stolen. Slyke's lawyer had come from Saratoga and had opened the small wall safe. Everything was in its place—papers, will, bank book, and a good sized sum of money. But of evidence as to a motive for the crime, there was none.

Bartley had learned also that there was ill feeling between Miss Potter and the chauffeur, and he had questioned her about it. She refused to say what it was, and seemed to consider Bartley's presence as an intrusion. He had secured nothing new from her. When asked if she knew whether Slyke had any enemies who might want to take his life, she replied she did not. Repeated questioning could not shake her story that the step daughter Ruth had not been expected home that night, and that she had not known the girl was in the house until we had all heard her voice on the stairs. As the girl carried her own key, she could easily, she said, have returned without her knowing it.

Then there was the dog to be considered. He had slept as usual in the big living room on the night of the crime. The girl's story of his walking to the foot of the stairs with her when she came in, proved that he was there the entire night. Bartley remarked that it was very strange that the dog should have made no sound.

"It looks," I commented, "as if whoever committed the crime did not pass through the living room."

Bartley gave me a disgusted look. "Or else, Pelt, the dog knew him. The only way to reach the room where Slyke slept was up those stairs, and to reach the stairs he had to pass through the living room. Remember this, too, Lawrence said that Slyke was not going to bed, but expected another visitor. The butler says the dog was in the room with him when he let Lawrence out. Suppose the other visitor came. If Slyke himself admitted him, the dog would have probably barked at least once— that is, unless he knew him."

"Then it might have been someone in the house," I suggested.

Bartley assented, and we discussed the various persons in the household. First, we both agreed that the shot the boy had heard was the one that had killed Slyke, and that the time must have been between half past one and two o'clock. If that were so, then, when the girl came in about three o'clock, Slyke was already dead. Bartley was sure that it took at least thirty minutes to undress Slyke and get him down from the balcony to his room. If the shot that the boy heard was fired before two o'clock, then the girl would not be suspected, for she had not returned until three. We eliminated her.

Bartley passed over the women servants with the remark that none of them had courage enough to commit the murder. He next considered the butler, not because there was any definite evidence against him, but because he was in the house at the time of Slyke's death. It was plain that he had not liked his master. His reason for being out of bed at three o'clock in the morning might have been to see if he had locked the windows, as he said, and again it might not have been. At least, that he was up and about at that time, was proved by his having seen Ruth come in.

Bartley then analyzed the sister in law. He said he felt sure she was hiding something, for she had not been frank in telling what she knew, and seemed anxious to get him out of the house. Whether what she was withholding concerned Slyke's death or not he could not tell; but whatever it was, he was determined to discover it.

"Do you remember, Pelt," he asked, "that Currie told us she runs a Ouija board? There is nothing startling in that; thousands are doing the same thing. Since the war all forms of spiritualism have made hundreds of converts. When she met King at the door this morning, she told him that the board had spelled 'trouble' the night before."

I stared at him in astonishment. He seemed to be regarding a Ouija board seriously. He saw my look and chuckled.

"Oh, I am not interested in the Ouija board itself; what I am interested in is that word 'trouble' that it spelled out for her."

This was more astonishing still, and I asked, "Why, you haven't any faith in those things, have you?"

Again he chuckled, then became serious. "Sure I have, but not in the way you think. You know what those boards are. They are made of ordinary pine, varnished, and the alphabet stamped on. They cost a few cents to make, but sell for over a dollar. People use them, thinking they are brought in touch with the dead and can receive messages from them."

"I know they do," I repeated, wondering what was the matter with him.

"The messages people think come from another world, come from the subconscious minds of the persons who are fooling with the board. They do not realize that they themselves are subconsciously directing its movements and spelling out their own messages. Now that board wrote for Miss Potter, 'Trouble is coming,' not once but many times. What I want to know is this: What was the something that, deep in her mind, told her that trouble was coming? What was the cause of her fear?"

He lighted another cigar before he continued, "There is still another thing that shows she knew some danger was threatening. You remember she also told us that she had dreamed that Slyke had been killed."

I knew what he was driving at now. Freud, whose theory of psycho analysis was well known to Bartley, had worked out the interpretations of dreams. At first his theory was smiled at, but today it is being accepted by scientists the world over. The theory of psycho analysis is that in our sleep the subconscious mind has full play; our repressions come to the surface and express themselves in dreams. The psycho analyst is thus often able to explore the secret places of our minds through them and tell the cause of our trouble. Bartley had once solved a murder from clues given him by the dreams the murdered man had before his death; and I realized now why he was so interested in Miss Potter's sleeping and waking dreams.

"Shakespeare was right when he said, 'We are such stuff as dreams are made of," he added in a quizzical tone as he paused to relight his cigar. "Miss Potter dreamed more than once that Slyke had been killed. We are told a dream is a suppressed wish, and that in our dreams our wishes are often hidden by symbols. The dream of death, for instance, is very common. Children often use the expression, 'I wish I were dead,' or they say, 'I wish you were dead.' A child simply means, 'I wish you were away so that I could do as I choose.' Death to the child does not mean physical death, but simply being absent. It is the same in the dreams of older people. They are often in the old symbolism of childhood. This woman probably did not wish Slyke actually dead. She had no quarrel with him as far as I know. What she did wish was entirely different. She wished that he might be away so that he would be out of some trouble, and her suppressed wish caused her to dream that he was dead. That's the reason why I believe that she knows more than she will tell."

"What can it be?" I asked.

"I don't know, but it is something that was causing a great deal of trouble to Slyke, perhaps to all of them. It might even be something that will bring dishonor. Anyway, it was so serious that, sleeping or waking, it was on her mind. I wish she would talk; we need all the light we can get."

"But that does not actually prove that she knows anything about his death," I suggested.

Bartley turned quickly and glanced at me to see if I were serious. Seeing that I was, he explained, "I don't say that it does. The Ouija board performances and the dreams were before his death, not after it. Of course, the fact that the dog did not bark throws suspicion on everyone that was in the house at the time."

He was silent for a while, glancing thoughtfully out of the window, and then resumed his story.

After I left him, he had locked himself in the tower for over an hour and gone over the two rooms and the balcony almost inch by inch. The only thing that had escaped us in our first search, he said, was a small stopper, the end covered with red wax. He was not sure whether the finding of the stopper meant anything or not. His second examination had made him more positive than ever that Slyke had been murdered, and that the murderer wished his death to appear to be suicide.

It would be almost impossible to make a jury believe that it was murder on the slight evidence that we had, and I said as much to Bartley. He agreed with me, and admitted he would not be surprised if King, as coroner, brought in a verdict of suicide. I pondered on this a while; then a thought struck me.

"Suppose, after all, he did kill himself, Bartley. You base your theory of murder on the position of the bed clothes and the way the gun was held. Suppose he did kill himself, and some other person, not the murderer, came into the room and pulled the bed clothes up around his neck."

He shook his head in denial. "We would still have, Pelt," he said with a rather sarcastic smile, "the other questions to be answered. First, we would ask how the blood stains got on the balcony of the tower. We would also want to know why the hand did not grasp the gun as tightly as it should. Then we would demand to know why there was no blood on the pillow where his head rested. It won't do. There is no doubt of it. He was killed."

I interrupted to ask if, as Miss Potter admitted, she had closed his eyes, why she might not have been also the one who pulled the bed clothes up around his neck.

Bartley replied, "It is true that she did close his eyes, but she insists she touched nothing else."

"But," I broke in, "what was her real reason for doing it?"

"She said, you remember, that the eyes frightened her. Let a nervous woman come suddenly upon a dead body and it is very possible that the eyes staring at her might so frighten her that she would close them. Her confession cleared up a point that bothered me. The accounting for the eyes being closed does not prove that he committed suicide, however. There is little enough evidence one way or another, but what there is points to murder and to nothing else."

"There is another thing," I said. "Why was the revolver taken from him while we were upstairs? It seems a very foolish thing to have done. Who did it? Was it the butler or Miss Potter?"

Both the butler and Miss Potter had been out of the tower room, Bartley reminded me, for some time before we suspected Slyke's death was murder and not suicide. As to who had taken the revolver, it was impossible to say as yet. If we believed that the butler had seen Briffeur on the stairs while we were on the balcony, then he might be the one. The finding of the gun in the vault and his appearance almost immediately afterwards seemed to point to Mm. Whoever had done it, had been very foolish.

After a pause he added that, so far, we had discovered no motive for Slyke's death. No one knew of any enemies that he had, nor did the investigation of the house and tower throw any light on it. Until we had found a motive for his murder, we should not be able to get very far in solving it. He continued in this strain for some time, jumping from one thing to another as he was apt to do in conversation. Many people wonder why he does not stick to one topic until he has exhausted it; but I know that, when he goes from one subject to another that is seemingly unconnected, he does it because he has found some relationship between them that we cannot see.

The next matter that he spoke about did not seem to have any relation with what had preceded it. It was the robbery of the year before. He had learned from the stepdaughter Ruth that she had not positively identified the men now in jail, but had thought that one of the men was similar in height and build to one of the men she had seen in the room. The room had been too dark for her to see very clearly. Nor was that all that she had told him which had disagreed with the accounts of the burglary that Rogers had given us. He had said that she had aroused Slyke and told him that burglars were downstairs; while in her story to Bartley she stated that, after she heard the noise in the living room, she went to the door of Slyke's room to call him, but found it empty. When she saw him he was standing on the lower step of the stairs leading to the living-room. There had evidently been a struggle, and a gun went off just before she reached him. It was she who had called the police, and Slyke had opposed her doing so "as nothing had been taken."

"You see how it looks, Pelt," he said with a grin. "Slyke did not want the police in at all. He did not wish any action taken, either then or later. He was nearer the men than anyone else, yet he swore he could not identify them. That makes me believe that he knew who they were and did not want the matter looked into."

"Did the girl tell you who found that piece of newspaper?" I asked.

"She said it was the chauffeur who had called their attention to it. The police do not seem to have made any search that night, or in fact until noon the next day. Then, with the help of the chauffeur and the butler, they searched the living room, and the chauffeur directed their attention to a piece of paper lying on the floor, half under a rug. Of course, you see what that leads us to. For hours that room had been unguarded, and anyone who wished could have gone in there. Even the piece of cloth was not found for several days, strangely enough; nor did the police find the footprints under the window until three days later, although they claimed they had searched the spot before."

I broke in with, "That looks, in other words, as if—"

"As if someone wished to send those men to jail," he finished for me.

He sighed, gave a little laugh, and remarked, "There are at least three things I would like to know. First, was the robbery a plant?"

"A plant?" I asked, looking at him in wonder.

"Yes! There may have been no robbery at all."

"What do you mean by that?"

He threw out his hands. "I don't quite know myself, but let that pass. There is another thing that puzzles me, and that is the chauffeur. I can tell by the way Miss Potter acted when we mentioned his name that she does not like him. He it was who took from the library the book with the account of the English crime in it. He had words with Slyke the day before his murder, and was missing when we wanted to question him. A few minutes after he was seen near the tower room the revolver was missing. I believe he is well worth watching. And lastly, what was the motive for Slyke's murder?"

A wild thought struck me. I knew at the time how absurd it was, yet a desire to hear what Bartley would reply made me voice it.

"Perhaps, the girl killed him."

Bartley gave me a surprised look, started to speak, then decided to wait and hear what I had to say.

"You say," I suggested, "that Slyke was killed about two o'clock in the morning. The girl might have come to the house and killed him; then gone back to her uncle's, and told the story about being afraid to go through the woods alone. She said it was three o'clock when he came with her to the house. That's a good alibi, of course; but suppose she had been to the house once before. The dog didn't bark because he knew her. She was also in the house when the revolver disappeared. If you claim the taking of the gun was foolish, why can it not be said to be the kind of an illogical thing a woman would do? The average man would know it was no use to remove the gun. You remember how startled the aunt was when she saw the girl."

Bartley had listened with an amused smile that grew broader as I talked. Though I had not been serious when I began, the more I thought of the idea the more plausible my suggestion sounded. Bartley himself had said that in the case we must build up a theory first, and then see if the facts would fit it.

When I had ended, he said that he himself had, at first, considered the possibility of the girl's having done it, but had decided against it. He reminded me that Slyke had been killed on the balcony, and carried down two flights of stairs, and that Slyke weighed one hundred and fifty pounds, the girl not a hundred. Remembering that and the task it was to carry such a heavy weight down so many stairs, did I still think the girl could have done it? Then in a rather sarcastic tone he mentioned other wild theories I had advanced in previous cases, theories that had proven in the end to have had nothing on which for me to base them.

My face turned red with chagrin, and, seeing that I was hurt, he smiled at me kindly and apologized.

"I didn't intend to hurt your feelings, Pelt. You are like all newspaper men, you enjoy building up a story out of nothing. In this affair, we mustn't let ourselves get sidetracked. We shall need all the clear thinking we can do."

Anxious to redeem myself, I said, "John, we have been going on the theory that someone from outside came into the house and killed Slyke, a mysterious visitor who arrived after Lawrence had left. Perhaps, the murderer was hiding in the house all the time."

He gave me an interested look and an approving nod.

"Suppose," I went on, "that the murderer was on the balcony. It was a good place to hide. It was so dark up there that he could not have been seen from the ground. Then let us assume that Slyke heard a sound above him, when he was in the room below the balcony, and went up to see what it was. The person may have made the sound on purpose to attract his attention. At any rate, when he does come out on the balcony, he is killed."

Bartley did not speak for a while, turning my suggestion over in his mind. Then he answered, "You may be right. It is possible that someone was waiting for him to come upstairs. But do not forget that, if that is so, the person would have had to wait there a long time; for he could not tell when Slyke would come into the room below the balcony. Still, your suggestion is well worth keeping in mind."

Although he spoke so favorably of my idea, I could see that he did not really agree with me.

I yawned and Bartley glanced at his watch. It was after three, and we should have been in bed several hours ago. He rose, and taking two objects from his pocket placed them on the desk. I leaned over to see what they were.

Lying black and sinister on the dark mahogany surface were the revolver that had been taken from Slyke's hand and hidden in the vault, and a little cork stopper, its end covered with red wax that showed where a knife had been used on it.

"Look," Bartley said, pointing at them with a laugh. "The sole results of a day's work. The only clues we have are before us. One is a revolver that did not have a finger print on it; the other a little stopper that might have come from anywhere. From these we have to discover the murderer."

Again he laughed. I stood looking at the two objects, thinking how insignificant they were and wishing they could speak and tell their story. Catching my mood, his face grew grave. He stood looking at them for a moment, then with a sudden gesture swept them into a small box saying. "We ought to have been in bed hours ago."

I had reached my room and was pulling down the bed covers when he called to me. I returned to his room and found him sitting on the edge of his bed taking off his shoes.

"I forgot to tell you, Pelt, that when we reach the solution of this murder, somehow or other whiskey will be mixed up with it. When you told me that Slyke had been selling whiskey to his friends, I knew that something was wrong. The finding of the liquor in his own vault makes me more certain. He must have known that that whiskey was there. Why, under heaven, a man that had the money Slyke was presumed to have had, should secrete whiskey on his grounds is more than I know."

"But," I reminded him, "you say he did not have as much money as people thought he had."

"Yes, that is true. The lawyer confirmed what I had heard about his losses. Whiskey and Slyke had a good deal in common, you will find."

He yawned, and I started again for my room. As I reached the door he added, "Black thinks the chauffeur killed Slyke. Maybe he did. Still"—and he laughed—"I never saw a man with a square head that knew very much. And that detective certainly has a square head."

And with that absurd remark in my mind, I went to bed.

VIII. The Inquest Opens

IT was only natural, after the lateness of the hour at which I went to bed, that I should oversleep the next morning. It was well after nine before I entered the breakfast room; I found no one there but a servant who told me that the others had eaten some time before. When I had finished my breakfast I went in search of Bartley, and found him in the sun parlor surrounded by a mass of newspapers. He waved to me and went on reading.

Picking up one of the papers, I sank into a chair by his side. I was curious to know what the New York papers had to say about Slyke's death. In the past he had furnished them with many a news item, and I knew that they would give him a good deal of space. I was surprised to find that they said little about the crime itself, but contented themselves with telling how he had killed himself, and in giving an account of his business career. The "*Record*" had one item of interest, however. After saying that Slyke had lived for many years in New York City, it added that, during the past two years, he had made his home entirely at Circle Lake. All of the papers made much of the robbery of the year before, and told of the effort being made to have the men pardoned.

The inquest was not to be held until one o'clock; and, as I laid my paper aside, I wondered what Bartley wanted me to do with my morning. As if in answer to my thought, he looked up and said he was going into Saratoga on some errands, and suggested that I go with him and interview the girl friend with whom Ruth had intended to spend the night. As Currie was occupied about the farm, we started off without telling him of our departure.

The first place we stopped on our arrival in town was at a large drug store, where Bartley asked to see the proprietor. When he appeared, Bartley placed a small object on the counter before him.

"Can you give me any idea," he asked, "what sort of a bottle that cork came from?"

The object was the little stopper with the red wax which he had showed me the night before. Picking it up, the druggist looked at it very carefully. He turned it over in his hand, scratched the wax with a knife, and took so long in replying that I thought he never would speak.

"I think I can," he said at last. "The little cork not only had its top covered with red wax, but the wax ran down the sides of the bottle. In order to get it open, it was necessary to cut the wax away. It looks to me as if it came from a Park Graham bottle."

"You mean the drug firm?" Bartley asked.

"Yes. I will show you."

He went behind the screen and returned in a second with a little bottle in his hand. It was but a few inches long, and the cork stopper was covered in the same manner with red wax, and part of it had run down the sides of the bottle. It was the mate to the stopper that Bartley had found. Bartley examined the bottle carefully, noted the label, and returned it to the druggist.

When we were again in the automobile, Bartley said, "I wish I were as sure what that stopper was doing in that room as the druggist is of the kind of a bottle it came out of."

Bartley's real object in coming to town was, however, to visit the jail and find out from Roche whether the chauffeur had told what he knew or not. I left him at the jail door, promising to return within an hour, and went in search of the young woman with whom Slyke's stepdaughter had expected to spend the night.

When I found her, Miss Morton bore out all that Ruth had said about the way she had happened to go home the night of the murder. They had been to a dance together, and on the way back the car had broken down near the entrance to the Slyke estate. Ruth said, as she was so near, she might as well go home. One of the young men had gone with her to the little cottage where her uncle, as she called the old minister, lived. He had waited until the old man had come downstairs, and had then rejoined his party. Ruth's story had been true, and I saw how very foolish my suggestion to Bartley had been that she might have committed the murder.

When I returned to the jail, about an hour later, I found that Bartley had gone to Doctor King's office, and I followed him there at once. It was the usual physician's office, with cases of instruments along the walls and a flat top desk in the center of the room. Bartley and the doctor were bending over a small pad when I entered, and Bartley told me that the doctor had been drawing for him a little map of the roads around the Slyke estate. The doctor looked older than when I had seen him first, far more tired and nervous. It took several years to get over shell shock, he told us, and he had been very foolish to start to practice again so soon after his return from the front. He recounted a few of his war experiences, and they were enough to have broken any man. He said that, as soon as his duties in regard to the Slyke case were over, he was going to take a rest. All the time he talked to us he played with a pencil or tapped the desk in front of him.

We spoke of the inquest, and he told us that he did not need to call a coroner's jury unless he wished. The facts were so complex or so simple—it was hard to say which—that a jury would be confused by them. He admitted that there was no doubt that Slyke had been murdered, but doubted if any jury would bring in a verdict of murder on such slight evidence as we had. He suggested that, if it were murder, someone from Saratoga might have committed the crime. He reminded us that the racing season was near, and that it always brought to the town a number of petty criminals from other cities.

One of them might have committed the crime. It was not a bad suggestion, and to my surprise Bartley seemed to regard it favorably. The doctor mentioned the chauffeur's arrest, and said that he had only known the man by sight. We talked for an hour or more, then returned home.

Bartley was in his room changing his suit for luncheon, when a telephone call came for him. When he returned he told me that the call had been from Mr. Slyke's lawyer. He had 'phoned him, Bartley said, that among the papers in the safe was an envelope with ten thousand dollars in bills in it, and that the bank had informed him that, on the day of our arrival, Slyke had deposited thirteen thousand dollars with them.

While this was interesting news, I could not see that it was of any importance to us, and said as much to Bartley. He half smiled as he reminded me that ten thousand dollars was a lot of money to keep in the house, and added that it was strange that Slyke should deposit thirteen and retain another ten in his house. He wondered if his keeping the money had any relation to the visitor that he was expecting. At any rate the man had not gotten the money, if that had been what he was after.

The luncheon bell rang at this moment; and, as we hurried downstairs, Bartley added, "At least we can't say Slyke committed suicide because of money troubles."

Luncheon over, Currie, Bartley and I started for the inquest. We hurried through the woods. The sun, which had been shining brightly all morning, had vanished, and miles away on the horizon great heavy, angry looking thunder clouds were rolling up. Long before the inquest would be over, I knew we would be in for a big thunder storm.

The newspapers had evidently received a tip that there was more in Slyke's death than had appeared, for when we arrived we were forced to run a gauntlet of reporters, who recognized Bartley at once and crowded around him. They realized that, if he were interested in the case, it was of more importance than they had suspected, and wanted to know if he did not have some information to give them. With a laugh at their insistence, he replied that he did not; but, when he had, he would see that they were the ones to get it.

There were a number of cars in front of the house and a small crowd of men standing about in twos and threes. Just as we turned to mount the steps, Lawrence drove up and greeted us with a rather forced smile.

The inquest was to be held in the large living room in which the burglars had been found. Though it was not a public hearing open to every one, there were a goodly number of people present. The room was filled with chairs, and the desk, which had stood in the center of the room, was now placed near one of the windows, with a chair behind it and a small table by its side.

Doctor King and the other officials had not yet arrived; and Black, who was talking to a group of men, left them and came to greet us. He told us that the chauffeur, Briffeur, was to be brought from the jail by Roche, and that he thought his testimony would make a sensation. Bartley seemed to understand what he meant, though I did not. The chauffeur had refused to talk and had answered all questions by saying that he would tell what he knew at the inquest. All attempts to find out what that might be had failed.

Bartley asked Black if he still thought that the chauffeur was guilty of the murder. Black countered by stating that he did not believe that anyone else knew as much about the affair as he did. It was his opinion that, if the chauffeur had not killed him, he at least knew something about the crime. One thing the man had admitted when questioned, and that was that, when he testified, he would ruin several reputations. Bartley was much interested, and told Black that he wished he would ask Roche not to bring Briffeur into the court room until it was time for him to give his testimony.

"Want to spring him?" asked the detective with a grin.

Bartley nodded, and Black went away to arrange the matter. I could see what Bartley was after. Only the police and ourselves knew that the man was to be placed on the stand, and Bartley wanted to see what effect his sudden introduction might have on those present. There might be someone so surprised by it that he would give himself away.

The room was filling rapidly. Most of the men seemed to be men of importance from the summer colony. Hardly any of them were people who lived all the year round at Circle Lake or in Saratoga. The district attorney, a clean cut man of forty, came in, followed by several assistants. As a rule, the district attorney of a county does not appear at a coroner's inquest, and his presence here showed that he thought the case an important one. Bartley went over to him, and the two men talked for several minutes, the district attorney nodding his head at the end, as if agreeing with something that Bartley had said.

By the time Bartley returned to my side again, the room was filled and the doors had been closed. At the one leading into the hall a policeman was stationed. The reporters were placed half way down the room, and the district attorney and his assistants at the small table with their stenographer. The room darkened as the storm came nearer and someone turned on the electric lights. Bartley moved his chair to one side so that he could watch all that went on and have the light fall full upon the faces of the witnesses as they testified.

In a row of chairs, directly in front of the coroner's desk and about six feet away, were seated the members of Slyke's household. Slyke's stepdaughter Ruth, dressed in dark blue, was between Miss Potter and an old man, who, I decided, was the minister uncle who had brought her home the night of the murder. I could not see Miss Potter's face, but her hands showed a great nervous strain; they were never still, picking incessantly at the folds of her dress. On her right were two empty chairs for the chauffeur and Roche, and beyond them the butler and the other servants.

We had to wait some time for the doctor, who had been delayed by a case. When he arrived, he pushed his way hurriedly through the people at the far end of the room, pausing only for a moment to speak to the district attorney. He took his place back of the desk, and, after removing some papers from his bag, stood for a moment looking over the crowd. He seemed almost too worn and nervous to preside.

A silence fell on the room, the curious, expectant silence that I have so often noticed at inquests. To most of the people present, the doctor had ceased to be their familiar friend and had become an impersonal officer of the law, the instrument for unraveling a mysterious death. Perhaps, some were thinking of the man in whose house they were and whose dead body lay above awaiting burial. The silence was suddenly broken by a heavy peal of thunder. The storm was almost at hand.

To my surprise, the doctor called as his first witness Slyke's sister in law. As a rule, the first person called at an inquest is the one who discovered the body, but for some reason the doctor had decided to keep the butler for a later moment. Miss Potter took the chair near the desk, sitting nervously on the edge of it, her face white, her eyes glancing restlessly over the room, then down at her feet.

The first questions, after she had taken the oath, were the usual ones. They related to her name and her relationship to Slyke. She said her name was Alice Potter, and that she was the sister of his dead wife. Slyke had asked her to come and run his house for him, and for the last ten years she had done so. In response to a question as to whether she had been paid for her services, she flushed deeply and explained that while no real salary had been paid, whenever she had needed money she had asked Slyke for it and he had given it to her. The sum varied, though she doubted if she had ever received more than a thousand in any one year. He always had been willing to give her as much as she asked for, and had not questioned the amounts. There had never been any trouble over money matters between them.

This was all evidence that I knew; and, while she was giving it, I glanced about the room, then watched the doctor. He was finding his position a very difficult one as he was the family physician as well as the coroner. He put his questions with as much delicacy as possible. The whole affair seemed to be very distasteful to him. It was particularly trying for a man who was still feeling the effects of a nervous breakdown. Miss Potter, fortunately, became more at ease as the questioning proceeded. She kept her eyes down and gave her answers in such a low voice that at times it was hard to hear them at all.

All through the early part of her evidence there were rumbles of distant thunder. Leaning back in my chair, I pushed aside the heavy draperies that hid the window, and looked out. It was almost like night. The sky was filled with heavy clouds and the rising wind lashed the tops of the trees. A big storm was close at hand. The thunder was still some miles away, and I could see distant, almost continuous flashes of lightning. After a quick glance I let the curtain fall back into place.

When I turned my attention again to the evidence, Doctor King was questioning Miss Potter about the finding of the body. She testified that she was at breakfast when the butler rushed into the room, crying that something was wrong with Mr. Slyke. She knew her brother in law had intended to go fishing that morning, and was surprised to learn that he was not yet up. The butler had told her that he had called him, and receiving no reply had entered his room and found Mr. Slyke still in bed. When he did not answer when spoken to again, he (the butler) had come at once to her.

She hesitated for several moments, unnerved by the memory of what she had seen; then, recovering her composure, she stated that she had gone up at once to his room, the door of which had been left open by the butler when he rushed out. She had crossed to the bed and called him by name. When he did not answer, she looked closer and saw that he was dead. Her voice broke a little on this last statement, but she soon recovered and continued. The next thing she had done, she said, was to call the doctor.

For the first time, the district attorney took a hand in the proceedings.

"Did Mr. Slyke ever lock his door at night?" he asked.

"Yes, sir; usually," was the reply.

"Tell us how you found him."

She answered that he was lying on his back, the bed clothes pulled up around his chin, and his hands by his side. She had not pulled the bed clothes down from the body, nor disturbed them in any way. It was not until she had noticed the wound in his head that she realized he had been shot.

"Did you disturb the body?" was the next question.

There was a long silence, then haltingly, "I—well, that is—I did close his eyes. Their expression frightened me, so—I—closed them."

She received a rather disgusted look from the district attorney, who asked, "Did you not know that the body should have been left as you found it?"

"I–" she made an appealing gesture, "I never thought of that. Only of his eyes! They frightened me, they— stared so. I simply closed them. But I did nothing else."

King then asked a question that surprised me. "You thought he had committed suicide?"

She hesitated, started to speak, stopped, and at last found her voice. "Why, yes. That— that is—I did at the time. But I don't know what to think now."

"Why did you think he killed himself?"

This seemed a harder question to answer than the other.

"Why, I don't know. You see, he was shot; and I knew of no one who would want to kill him. As far as that goes, I know of no reason why he should have wanted to take his own life."

The next questions were along the line she had suggested by her answers. Could she not think of some reason why he might have committed suicide, ill health or money troubles? Had he quarreled with anyone lately. She seemed to have more difficulty with these last questions than with any of the previous ones. She was so long in answering that some of them had to be repeated several times. She was so careful of what she said that she gave me the impression that she was trying to keep something back.

In response to the first question, she repeated that she knew no reason why Slyke should want to commit suicide. She had heard of no money troubles, and his health was good. No, she had never heard of his having quarreled with anyone. It was this last answer that she had hesitated longer over than over any of the others, and it was the one which caused me to feel sure she was hiding something.

The question regarding the revolver that had been found in Slyke's hand she answered readily enough. He had kept it in his room, just where, she did not know; it was one that he had bought a year before.

When questioned as to her own doings on the night of his death, she could tell us nothing of value. There had been a card party, but she had gone to bed about ten o'clock and had not even heard the men go out. During the night she had heard no sound. As this was all she had to tell she left the stand. Though her testimony had thrown no light on what had taken place, I felt more strongly than ever that she could have done so had she wished. I glanced at Bartley, and the queer smile he gave me hinted that he, too, thought as I did.

The next witness was a Doctor Webster. I knew that a second physician had been called in on the morning of the crime, but had not met him. Doctor King's position was a peculiar one, as he was not only the physician who had first seen the body, but also the coroner. In order to have the testimony of a second medical man, he had sent Doctor Webster to examine the body and testify as to its condition. As the doctor took the seat near the coroner, I examined him closely. He was a man of at least sixty, rather stout, with a beaming, kindly face, and white beard that gave him the appearance of a practitioner of the old school.

In response to questions, he told how Doctor King had requested him to go to the house and examine the body, because, as coroner, King himself could not testify at the inquest. In terms more scientific than plain, he described how Slyke met his death, a death which, he said, must have been instantaneous as the bullet had lodged in the brain.

"Doctor, do you think the wound could have been self inflicted?" came the question.

The doctor paused, then answered thoughtfully, "That is very hard to answer. So far as the wound itself is concerned, it could have been self inflicted. But other things that were brought to my attention cause me to believe that it could not have been so inflicted."

The room stiffened into attention. It was the first hint they had had that Slyke might have been murdered.

"Explain your answer. What do you mean by other things that were brought to your attention?' "

The doctor replied slowly, "The facts I will mention were brought to my attention by Mr. John Bartley, the famous criminal investigator, whom I found at the house when I arrived."

At the mention of Bartley's name a little murmur of surprise went over the room. His name seemed to be known to almost all present, and I saw men look at each other and several shake their heads as if to say that as Bartley was present Slyke's death must be more complex than they had supposed. Half way down the room the reporters, for the first time, were writing hurriedly, and in a second a telegraph boy went out with a mass of telegrams. Within an hour the fact that Bartley was working on the case would be in all the newspaper offices in New York.

The doctor continued, "Mr. Bartley aided me in making my examination of the body. The wound was, as I have said, one that a man could have easily inflicted upon himself, but such a wound causes death within a few seconds after it is made. I thought at first sight that it was suicide, but Mr. Bartley pointed out that the hands of the dead man, one of which held the revolver, were under the bed clothes and that they were pulled up smoothly around his neck. It would have been impossible for Mr. Slyke, himself, to have done that. I mean he could not have killed himself and then placed his arms under the clothes, after first pulling them up around his chin. He would not have had time before he died had he fired the shot. As Mr. Bartley pointed out— and as I should have thought of for myself—in cases of violent death the eyes are open. Mr. Slyke's eyes were almost closed. How they were closed after his death, Miss Potter has just told us."

Again there came a murmur of astonishment. The doctor's statement had been entirely unexpected by most of the audience. For the first time it was suggested that, instead of Slyke's having killed himself, he had been murdered. All awaited eagerly further developments.

"Then you would say that Mr. Slyke was murdered?" came the question.

The doctor's answer was a long time in coming.

"I hardly know what to say. What Mr. Mr. Bartley pointed out to me causes me to believe that Mr. Slyke was killed. Of course, there is a possibility that the wound might have been self inflicted, and someone else arranged the bed clothes around his neck after he was dead."

He paused again, then continued, "That might have been done, but the chances are that he did not kill himself. I cannot positively state, however, whether it was suicide or murder."

His hesitation started a long argument between him, the coroner, and the district attorney. If Slyke had killed himself, then someone else must have pulled up the bed clothes and arranged the body. What had been the person's reason for doing it? If, on the other hand, he had been murdered, then a very definite attempt had been made to make it look like suicide. The revolver in the dead man's hand came under discussion, and Doctor Webster said that, though it could be placed in a person's hand after death, any trained eye could detect the fact. After being on the stand for over thirty minutes, he was allowed to return to his seat.

His evidence, while it had for the first time suggested that a murder might have been committed, had yet done little to clear up the mystery. I could see by the doubt and bewilderment in their faces that his uncertainty as to whether it was murder or suicide had communicated itself to the audience. They looked eagerly about for the next witness, wondering what his testimony would disclose. There was little enough, as I knew too well, that any witness could tell that would throw light on Slyke's death.

The coroner glanced at a piece of paper and said, "Will Mr. John Bartley kindly take the stand?"

IX. The Cry In The Dark

THERE was a little stir of excitement as Bartley, with easy grace, arose and took his seat in the witness chair. Every one was eager to see him, and he became at once the center of all eyes. I do not know just what they had expected, perhaps the usual uneducated, rough detective; what they saw was a man dressed in a costly gray suit, with a keen, intellectual face and an air of good breeding. He leaned back in his chair with a little smile on his lips; testifying at inquests was no new experience to him.

Doctor King did not trouble Bartley with questions, but allowed him to tell his story in his own way. In a low, musical voice, he began his narrative with the telephone call he had received from Doctor King. He recounted our arrival at the house and our examination of the body. As he told of his reasons for thinking that Slyke had been murdered, the room became very still. He described our search for clues in the tower rooms, and what he had found on the balcony. Slowly the audience realized that Slyke had not been killed in any of the rooms of the house, but on a tower sixty feet in the air.

He pictured in short, concise words how the body had been carried down two flights of stairs, undressed and put into bed. A gasp went around the room at his words, and I could see from the faces of the listeners that they could scarcely believe the story he was telling them. The sensation was increased when he spoke of the removal of the revolver from the dead man's hand while we were in the upper room of the tower. This was, without a doubt, so far the most dramatic moment of the inquest.

The district attorney and the coroner did not question him after he had finished. There was no need to do so, for Bartley had apparently told them all that he knew. When he had taken his seat, I realized that he had not mentioned his reason for being at the Lake, nor had he said a word about the burglary of the year before. It seemed strange that every one should take his being present so much as a matter of course. The finding of the whiskey and the recovery of the revolver, which last I doubted if anyone but ourselves knew about, Bartley had also kept to himself. There was no direct evidence, of course, connecting Slyke with the whiskey, and it seemed to have nothing to do with the crime itself. That was probably why, I decided, that Bartley had not mentioned it.

While he had been giving his testimony, the storm had come nearer. In spite of the heavy draperies that were drawn over the long windows and the brilliant lighting of the room, we saw vivid flashes of lightning every now and then. As Bartley resumed his seat by my side, the thunder came in long, heavy peals that shook the house and I heard the trees lashing under the wind. A thunder storm is never a cheerful thing at the best, and this one was making everyone very uneasy. At each clap of thunder, someone would give a start and glance nervously around.

The next witness, the photographer, was only on the stand a short time. He told of taking the pictures of the room in which the body lay and of the body itself, and stated that he had seen no revolver in the dead man's hand.

The testimony of the following witness was also brief. The boy who worked around the garage, although very much frightened, stuck to his story that he was getting into bed when he heard a shot, and that it sounded as if it were up in the air. The time, he thought, was somewhere between two and three in the morning.

When he had returned to his seat the step-daughter took his place. Her youthful face flushed under the many eyes that were turned upon her, and she never looked up. Her story was the one that she had told to Bartley and she added nothing new to it. In answer to a question as to whether she had glanced at her stepfather's door when she passed it the night of the murder, she replied that she had and that it was closed. Catching the district attorney's eye at this point, Bartley motioned him to his side and they whispered together for a moment. The district attorney then asked the girl if she had seen the dog when she came in. Rather surprised at the question, she answered that the dog had met her at the front door, smelled of her dress, and followed her to the stairway before going back to his rug. When she left the stand, her testimony had not added anything to what we already knew.

I realized suddenly that we knew no more about the crime than we had when the inquest began. Though I was sure in my own mind that Slyke had been murdered, I had grave doubts if it could be proved satisfactorily to others. The almost entire absence of clues made it seem more mysterious than it had at first, if that were possible. Even the next witness, Mr. Lawrence, added nothing to our knowledge. He took his seat with the air of a man that was about to be punished for some indiscretion. His pale face flushed when he realized the number of eyes upon him, and he gave his evidence in a voice so low that at times the thunder, which was coming nearer, completely drowned it. It was exactly the same story that he had told me in his office. He said that, at the close of the party, Mr. Slyke had asked him to stay behind, for what he did not know at the time. After the others had left, Mr. Slyke had taken him up to his room in the tower, and had asked him if he would like to buy a little whiskey as he had more than he needed.

There was a ripple of laughter at this unexpected statement. Though it was the first time that whiskey had been introduced into the case, I doubt if anyone regarded its mention as important. The laughter made Lawrence more nervous than ever, and he talked faster and more indistinctly. He had stayed only a few moments, he said, though Slyke had urged him to remain longer. A moment after he had been released from the stand, I remembered that he had not mentioned the fact that Slyke had told him he was expecting another visitor. Whether Lawrence had forgotten it or did not wish to volunteer the information, I could not decide. It seemed to me to be a very important point for him to have omitted.

The butler, who came next, took his seat to the accompaniment of one of the worst claps of thunder that we had yet had, a clap that seemed almost in the room. Then a burst of rain swept against the windows. All through his testimony the thunder made it almost impossible to hear him, and he had to repeat many of his statements. He appeared to be a silent man who seldom spoke of his own volition. Something in his manner gave me the impression that he had not been very fond of Slyke, though just what it was I could not say. His face had the calm expression of a man accustomed to taking orders and fulfilling them without question. He had little to tell us and disposed of the card party in a few words. After it had broken up and he had let Mr. Lawrence out, he had locked the windows but left the front door unfastened as Mr. Slyke had told him that he, himself, would attend to it later. In answer to a question as to whether he had seen Slyke after Lawrence left, he replied that he had not. In fact, he had not seen him again alive. He had gone to his room, leaving the dog in the living room as was the custom. His first knowledge that Slyke was dead came when he entered his room with Miss Potter.

So far, like all the other witnesses that had been heard, his testimony presented nothing that we had not already known. Then suddenly he added a new piece of information. So far as we had been able to discover, the relations that had existed between Slyke and the members of his household had been the usual ones. I mean by that, that while there had been no unusual show of affection nor any signs of deep grief at his death, there had been no evidence of any trouble between them. When the butler was asked if he had ever heard words between Slyke and any member of his family, he surprised us all by saying that he had twice heard Miss Potter and the broker quarreling.

Miss Potter gave an angry start and turned a flushed face on the servant, who refused to meet her eyes. The girl by her side looked around at her aunt, startled. I glanced quickly at Bartley and saw an amused smile on his lips.

"You say you heard Miss Potter and Mr. Slyke quarreling?" asked the coroner.

The butler began to speak, but his words were drowned out by a terrific clap of thunder that shook the house. When the sound had died away in the distance he answered, "Why, yes, sir, I did; twice."

As he paused and did not continue, the coroner asked him to tell us where the quarrel had taken place and what it had been about. From the rather self satisfied expression on the butler's face, I judged that he was not only willing, but glad, to tell all that he had heard.

"It was one evening in the dining room," he stated, "right after dinner, and only Miss Potter and Mr. Slyke were in the room. As I was about to enter from the butler's pantry, I heard Mr. Slyke say in a loud voice, 'You make me sick.' Then came Miss Potter's voice, very angry, 'I do, do I? Never mind. You will be a lot sicker before you get through. I tell you, there is lots of trouble ahead of you.' That's all I heard, for they left the room by another door."

"Do you know what they were talking about?"

The butler was silent a moment, then shook his head without speaking.

"And when was the second occasion that you heard them quarreling?" he was asked.

"It was about a week later, I think. One morning, when I was passing Mr. Slyke's room, I heard them again. He seemed to be very angry about something, I don't know what. His voice was loud enough to be heard through a closed door, 'I wish you could keep your mouth shut. It's none of your business, anyhow.' Then I heard Miss Potter; she was angry also. 'You wait and see. It will be my business if you are not careful. If you keep on, something will happen to you.' "

This was an astonishing piece of information. After all, things had not gone as smoothly in the household as we had supposed. What the last expression, "And if you keep on, something will happen to you," might mean, I could not decide. It might have been a threat; and, in view of what had taken place, it would be necessary for Miss Potter to explain it. Glancing at her, I noticed that though angry and nervous she was not afraid. She seemed to regard what the butler had said as more annoying than accusing. When I looked at Bartley, he showed no surprise; but then I had scarcely expected that he would, for he made it a point never to be surprised at anything that might come up. The butler admitted that he did not know what the quarrel had been about, and that, with the exception of the two times he had mentioned, the relations that had existed between Slyke and his sister in law had always been very friendly.

The storm was now directly overhead. Claps of thunder were almost incessant, and vivid flashes of lightning penetrated the room in spite of the heavy curtains drawn over the windows. The house seemed to shake on its foundations. Several times the electric lights flickered away to a mere blur, while the flashes of lightning made the room as bright as noon day.

As the butler left the stand, there was a slight commotion in the rear of the room; and turning, I saw Roche making his way between the chairs pushing the chauffeur ahead of him. King gave the two men a puzzled glance, and then turned to the district attorney and whispered something to him. Miss Potter also turned to see what the noise was, and an expression of consternation and dread came over her face.

The two men passed within a foot of me, and the cruel lips and shifty eyes of the chauffeur made me wonder why Slyke should have kept such a man in his employ. When they reached the front of the room, Roche motioned the chauffeur to the empty chair next to Miss Potter, who drew as far away from him as she could, and then seated himself on the other side of his prisoner. The chauffeur gave her a look filled with hatred, blended with a smile of triumph. I could see that there was something wrong between these two.

A sharp peal of thunder seemed to split the air, causing the crowd to stir uneasily in their chairs. Again the lights flickered down for a moment, and again the thunder rolled. A violent wind lashed the rain against the windows behind me, and there was scarcely a pause between the flashes of lightning. The room was deathly still; we were petrified.

Doctor King was standing behind his desk, his face white, one hand playing nervously with the papers in front of him. I remembered that when we first met him, he had told us that the thing he disliked most was a thunder storm, and I could see that this one was rapidly unnerving him. He started at each vivid flash of lightning and the thunder seemed to daze him. Turning to the district attorney, and speaking half to him and half to the room, he said, "I think we should adjourn the inquest until tomorrow. The storm is so bad that I doubt if we can hear the testimony of the other witnesses."

His decision seemed to be very sensible. We had been unable to hear the close of the butler's evidence because of the thunder, and I doubted if any but those in the front seats would be able to hear the witnesses that were still to be called. The district attorney objected, however, to adjourning. He said that he could not be present the next day, and thought that we had better hear the remaining witnesses at once. Sinking back into his chair, King asked the attorney whom he wanted called next.

The district attorney rose to his feet, saying slowly, "I am going to call Briffeur, who was chauffeur for Mr. Slyke. He will– "

But whatever he was going to add we never discovered. Just at that second there came a terrific flash of lightning that seemed to burn its way across the room, followed by a deafening clap of thunder. With a sizzle the lights went out and left the room as black as the inside of a coal mine. Low murmurs came from all sides. It was enough surely to try the nerves of the most stout hearted.

As the rumble of thunder died away, I heard King demanding, in a voice that shook a little, "Will somebody get a light—lamps or candles?"

Someone pushed back a chair, and then suddenly, rising above all else and ringing through the room with a horror that seemed to glue me to my seat, came a shriek of terror. It was sustained for a second, then died away in a long, sobbing moan.

X. SUDDEN DEATH

FOR a moment after the cry had died away the only sound to be heard was the dashing of the rain against the windows and the lashing of the trees outside. Everyone was too startled and frightened to move. I felt Bartley's hand on my arm, his fingers sinking deep into my flesh. Then the spell was broken, and men asked each other in excited whispers what had happened.

The cry had seemed to come from the front of the room. It had been one of horror, dread and surprise, as if the person uttering it had met with some unexpected and awful experience. It had been a man's voice, and I wondered whose it could have been.

"Come on, Pelt."

Bartley pushed back his chair and half dragged me to my feet. "We started to grope our way between the chairs toward the place from which the cry had come. The room was still in darkness and our progress was very slow. Then the lights began to flicker very dimly, and suddenly flashed on again in all their power.

At first glance, there seemed to be nothing wrong; then I noticed that King was bending over his desk, his face dead white, his eyes fixed on something on the floor in front of him, and fear showing in every feature. I realized suddenly that the chauffeur's chair was empty, and that Roche was on his knees before some object. Miss Potter, who had also been staring at the floor, fainted and fell sidewise into the arms of her niece. Then I saw what was the matter: the chauffeur was lying on the floor, with his face white, and his eyes closed.

Bartley dropped to his knees beside Roche and gave one searching look at the man, then straightened up with a queer expression on his face. He pointed silently to the chauffeur. On his brown coat, slowly darkening and widening, was a splotch of blood, and from his heart protruded the hilt of a knife.

For a moment my head swam. Only a short time before the lights had gone out the chauffeur had had a self confident sneer on his face; now he was lying on the floor, white and still, a knife in his breast. Another murder had taken place in Slyke's house, and this time in a room crowded with people

The district attorney and Doctor Webster had by now reached our side, and the doctor knelt down by the chauffeur. With a glance at the excited crowd pushing its way toward us, Bartley suggested to Roche that he clear the room of all but the family. It was not until he had called some of his men to his aid that he was able to make the excited spectators obey his orders and withdraw. Doctor King was assisting Ruth to restore her aunt to consciousness. As for Bartley, myself and Black, who had come forward, we had eyes for nothing but the silent figure of the chauffeur.

Doctor Webster opened his coat and examined the wound. Then, when he had turned back his eyelids and felt his pulse, he slowly shook his head and said to Bartley, "He can't live more than five minutes. The knife reached his heart."

"Will he recover consciousness before he dies?" Bartley asked.

"I can't say. He might for a moment."

Even as he spoke the chauffeur opened his eyes, eyes that still retained their look of horror and dazed surprise. Weakly his glance traveled over the faces bending over him; he tried to raise one hand, but the effort was too much for him and his eyes closed again. When he opened them a second time, he seemed to recognize Bartley and gave him such an appealing look that he bent closer. His eyes had begun to glaze and his face to take on a waxen hue. Though his lips moved feebly, no words came from them. Then, with a final effort, he gathered up what little strength he had left, and, in a voice so low we could hardly distinguish the words, he stammered forth, "The—robbery—robbery. Those men—innocent, ask boy."

His voice died away and his eyelids sank; then he opened them again and gasped, "The—boy—he knows."

I saw Bartley's face lighten, but he did not speak. Briffeur lay so still that we thought he had ceased to breathe; but, as the doctor started to rise, he made a sudden effort to sit up, and Bartley put his arm under him. With eyes flashing, he cried in a loud voice, "Slyke—mur—murdered. I—" His arm rose from his side and pointed straight in front of him, his finger almost touching Doctor Webster who gazed down at him, puzzled. "I—killed—" The chauffeur's voice broke; his lips ceased to move; and, without even a sigh, his head fell back. The chauffeur would never speak again.

Silently we rose to our feet, and stood looking down at the dead man. We were all too overcome by what had taken place, to speak. It seemed impossible that a man could have been done to death in a roomful of people, with the chief of police on one side of him and three detectives near him. But murdered he had been. Bartley seemed to feel as dazed as I did; for he took the knife the doctor handed him, without looking at it, his eyes upon the chauffeur and on his face a very odd expression. None of us seemed fully able to grasp that a man had been murdered almost before our eyes.

Doctor King had been working over Miss Potter, and she now opened her eyes and glanced around wildly. She saw the body at her feet, and with a little cry asked, "What's happened?"

No one answered for a moment; and then Bartley replied simply, "Someone has murdered the chauffeur."

At the word murder she gasped and covered her eyes with her hand. After a moment she removed it, and stammered, "How—Who?"

No one attempted to answer. The truth was that no one could. All we knew was that he had been killed by the knife that was now in Bartley's hand. But how, why, and by whom it was done, none of us knew. It seemed incredible that anyone could have crept up to the murdered man in the dark without being heard by those seated on either side of him. His cry had lasted but the barest fraction of a second; it seemed scarcely time enough between the moment when the lights went out and the time when the cry came for anyone to have come up to him, murdered him, and gotten away again. The murder must have been committed by someone near him. On one side of him had been Miss Potter; and, on the other, Roche. Roche was above suspicion; a police chief does not kill his prisoner unless he attempts to escape. Then I remembered the strange look that had passed between Miss Potter and the chauffeur when the latter had entered the room.

Though there had evidently been ill feeling between the two, it seemed absurd to suppose that she had killed him. To have done it, she would have had to have known that he would be seated beside her. I knew that no one but the coroner had known beforehand how the witnesses would be placed. Nor could she have known that the lights would go out just when they did, and thus give a chance to strike the blow. It dawned on me, at this point, that she could not have known that the chauffeur would be called as a witness, and might not have even known that he had been arrested. Yet the blow had been struck by someone near her, and very near to him.

At this moment Roche hurried into the room, his fat red face flushed to an even redder hue, his eyes wide and curious.

"What shall I do with those people outside?" he asked the district attorney. "I got them out of the house, but the reporters are howling their heads off. They want to know what has happened."

The attorney gave Bartley an appealing look.

"If I were you," Bartley told him, "I would call the inquest off, for today at least. You have heard all the important evidence. What Briffeur might have said we shall never know. Our duty now is to try and discover what happened to the poor chap."

He turned to Doctor King. "If I were you, Doctor, I would take the name of everyone that was in the room this afternoon. You might tell the reporters, Roche, that we will talk to them later."

As both King and the district attorney nodded, Roche hurried from the room, but returned a moment later. Again we stood hesitating, no one seeming to know just what to do next, waiting for Bartley to take the lead. Seeing that we were depending on him, he walked to the desk where King had sat, and called us around him.

Silently he turned the knife over and over in his hand, then gave it to each of us in turn to examine. It was a curious kind of a knife, looking as if it had had hard usage. The handle was of wood, rather heavy, and the blade, some four inches long, came to a fine, sharp point. As the blade did not close, it was an awkward weapon to carry around, and I wondered where the murderer had hidden it. The more I looked at it, the more I wondered what it had been used for. It was not a hunting knife, although it somewhat resembled one, of that I was sure. In fact, it was unlike any knife that I had ever seen.

We all looked at it silently; and, when the last to handle it had placed it back on the desk, Bartley picked it up for a second time.

"This is the weapon that killed Briffeur. You wonder why I allowed you to touch it instead of keeping it for finger prints. You will find no finger prints; for whoever used it had sense enough to have his hand covered."

Suddenly I remembered that he had said the same thing about the murderer of Slyke. There had been no finger prints found in the rooms or on the revolver. I wondered if there could be any connection between the two deaths.

"It is, of course, significant," Bartley continued, his voice grave, "that this man was killed as he was about to testify. It looks very much as if someone in the room feared that he might tell who killed Slyke, and, to prevent it, took a great chance and killed him in a room full of people."

Doctor King, in a rather excited voice, broke in to say, "But, Mr. Bartley, no one could have known that the lights would go out. I myself did not ever know that Briffeur was to testify, and I doubt if anyone else did."

Bartley listened to the doctor's words with a grave face. "That is so, King. So far as I know, only Roche, Black, the district attorney, and myself knew that the chauffeur would testify. None of us knew, however, what he was going to say, for he had refused to tell us. It is absurd to think that any of us killed Briffeur. Pelt, Black and myself were at the rear of the room. The district attorney was at least seven feet away from him. The only person near him was our friend Roche."

The red face of the police chief turned even redder. In astonishment he hastily stammered, "My God, Mr. Bartley, you don't think I killed him, do you?"

Under any other circumstances his dismay would have been so humorous that we all would have laughed, but we had no desire to do so now. We all agreed with Bartley, when he assured him that no one had even thought for a moment that he had committed the murder. He added that his remark had been intended simply to show how mysterious the crime was.

"It seems almost incredible," he continued after a short pause, "that the chauffeur could have been killed while we were all in the room with him. But he has been, and we must find out who did it. I think the best thing to do will be for each of us to seat himself just where he was when the lights went out. But first, we had better remove the body."

Black, Roche, and Doctor Webster raised the chauffeur's body and carried him from the room, followed by Doctor King. While they were gone, Bartley got down on his knees before the chair in which the chauffeur had sat and examined the heavy dark blue carpet which covered the floor. He was searching for a clue, I knew, that would give a hint as to how the murder had been committed. Miss Potter and Ruth, who had resumed their old seats, watched him with white faces.

When he rose to his feet, Bartley stood looking silently down at the floor with a little frown on his face. At last he turned to me and said, "When Briffeur came into this room and took his chair, Pelt, he was, of course, facing the coroner and the district attorney. When we found him after the lights came on, he had sunk to the floor in a position directly opposite to that in which he was seated—that is, with his back to them. It may be that, at the moment of the blow, he had half turned to see what had happened to the lights, or he may have swung around after the blow as he was slipping to the floor."

I nodded, and he continued, "You notice the blow came very close to the center of the heart. The murderer knew where to strike. If his knife had reached the place aimed for, the chauffeur would have died without uttering a word. In fact—"

He was prevented from saying more by the return of the others. At his suggestion, they took the places they had occupied when the lights went out. I was asked to take the chair that Briffeur had been in. This placed Roche on my left, so near that I almost touched him, and Miss Potter about a foot away on my right. Doctor King took his station behind the desk, which was directly in front of me and about eight feet away. The chair of the district attorney was at his side. Black and Webster stood near Bartley, who had seated himself on the desk.

For several moments he glanced around the room, trying to re create for himself the way the row of chairs had looked when the lights had been extinguished. As his keen eyes studied us, a frown came to his face, lingered a second, then faded away.

"You people in the front row," he commented, "were the nearest to the chauffeur. If anything was heard, you would have been the ones to hear it. Of course, the rattle of the thunder would have drowned almost any other sound. The crowd was a bit uneasy, too, because of the sharp lightning, and made a little rustling noise of its own; yet it seems almost incredible that anyone could have crept up to Briffeur and struck him down without either Miss Potter or Roche having heard them."

Miss Potter flushed, and without waiting for him to say more she interrupted, "I never heard a thing; not a thing."

Bartley studied her carefully as he asked, "Are you sure?"

Her face paled, then the color returned, but again she replied, "I heard nothing until that horrible cry rang out."

I saw her shudder as if the memory of it were almost too much for her, but she continued bravely, "I knew it was beside me, and I wondered what had happened. It frightened me— so much—that I can't tell just what happened after that."

She seemed to be telling the truth; yet I could not understand how anyone had gotten near enough to Briffeur to kill him without the person next to him hearing his approach.

Bartley toyed with a piece of paper a second, then smiled as he said, "Of course, the cry startled you, Miss Potter. But before or after it came, can you think of no little occurrence that might help us? Nothing at all?"

She was silent for a long time, then slowly, as if apologetic, she answered, "That is, I heard nothing, but— I did think I felt something brush my dress—on the side next to Briffeur. I am not sure, however. I only thought something did. The next moment I heard him slip to the floor and knew something was wrong."

Bartley's eyes brightened at her remark, and he asked eagerly, "Can you show us just where your dress was brushed?"

She hesitated as if trying to collect her thoughts, and glanced down at her dark brown dress. Then she placed her hand on a spot a little above her waist line. Bartley came to her side and looked closely at the place she indicated, then suddenly knelt, his eyes close to the cloth. Straightening up, he pointed out to us a small splotch, a little darker than the goods of which the dress was made. With a significant glance he said one word, "Blood!"

At the word, a look of horror came into Miss Potter's face and she shrank away.

"Was that stain on your dress when you put it on?" he asked as he rose to his feet.

"No! The dress was worn this afternoon for the first time since it was returned from the cleaner's."

He said nothing more, but went back to the desk. I presume that we were all wondering what the blood stain indicated. The wild thought rushed over me that she might, after all, have killed Briffeur; but I dismissed it at once as impossible.

"Now, Roche," asked Bartley, "did you hear anything?"

Roche, of course, understood the importance of his answer; and his red face became cautious and his hands clenched. Then, very slowly, as if counting his words, he answered, "I don't know, Mr. Bartley, that I heard anything—that is, anything except the little sound the people, behind me made when the lights went out. If you mean, did I hear anyone creep up on that poor fellow, I did not. If anyone came near him, I should have at least heard something; but I did not hear anything like that."

"What did you hear?" asked Bartley, a shrewd smile on his face.

The chief actually blushed. In an apologetic tone he said, "Now—Mr. Bartley, I don't know if I heard anything. But I thought—"

"What did you think?"

Roche shrugged his shoulders, hesitated, then answered, "Why, I thought that, a second or so before he gave that cry, I heard—" He paused like a man who is afraid that what he is going to say will sound absurd. "I don't know just what to call it. It was very slight, more like a little thud. I could scarcely hear it. It sounded as if a small object had struck something."

The keen face of Bartley was eager, and he leaned forward, his eyes on Roche's face. "And that was just before he cried out?" he asked.

"Yes, only a second before. It was just after I thought I heard something else."

Bartley demanded, "what?"

The chief hesitated again, pausing as if to think out carefully what he wished to say.

"Why—Mr. Bartley, when that last clap of thunder came, I thought the house had been struck, and was so upset that I don't know if I really heard anything at all. What I thought I heard sounded like a bough moving in the wind, or the whir of a violin string."

His description was so vague that we looked at each other, puzzled. Bartley tried to make the chief more definite, but to all his questions he received the same reply. Roche was not sure if he had heard anything, but if he had, it had sounded like a bough in the wind. What it was, or what had caused it, he had not the faintest idea.

Failing to get a more definite description from him, Bartley asked him to tell what happened after he heard the slight thud. The chief replied that the next thing he heard was the chauffeur's cry. It had been so sudden and terrifying that for a moment he had not moved. Then he had felt Briffeur fall against him; and before he could steady him, he had slipped to the floor. He had knelt at once beside him, and was, by feeling, trying to find out what had happened to him, when the lights had flashed on again; and he saw that Briffeur was lying on his back with a knife in his chest.

That was all he could tell us. That Briffeur could have been killed with Roche within a few inches of him—killed by someone who did not make a sound—seemed impossible. Yet it had been done. I concluded that the thud he had heard was the sound of the knife being driven into the body, but I could not account for the sound of the bough. The chief might have imagined that he heard it, or have been confused by the movements of the alarmed crowd behind him.

Bartley questioned the others. Ruth, her face pale, trembled a little as she answered that she had heard nothing but the cry. The district attorney replied that he had heard nothing else, either, and had not dreamed that a crime had been committed until he saw the figure on the floor. Doctor King's answer was similar. The impossible had happened. Briffeur had been murdered, not only without anyone near him hearing the murderer, but without his leaving any traces behind him.

As person after person denied having heard a sound, Bartley's face became grave. Later, he told me he agreed with my belief that the murderer could not have crept up on the chauffeur without making at least some slight noise. When all had finished, he gave a little shrug, and a faint smile came to his lips. I would have given a good deal to know what had caused it.

"Whoever struck that blow," Doctor Webster commented, "knew where to place it. The slightest fraction of an inch nearer, and the chauffeur would have died instantly. The darkness probably caused the murderer to miss the exact spot he was aiming for—the center of the heart."

Bartley agreed, and for a moment nothing more was said. Then the district attorney broke the silence with, "Mr. Bartley, I think that Briffeur knew who killed him. At least, he had an idea who it was. He was trying to tell us when he died."

"Yes," Bartley replied with a curious smile, "he was not only trying to tell us, but to point him out. You will remember that just before he died, in a last burst of strength, he half raised himself and said, 'Slyke murdered—I— killed—' and fell back dead. There is no doubt he thought he knew who killed him. He had not, of course, seen who it was. But he suspected someone, and was trying to point him out."

"Trying to point him out?" echoed the district attorney in astonishment.

"Yes, point him out. He pointed straight at Doctor Webster's chest."

The doctor started and his face reddened in surprise and anger. He glanced quickly at Bartley to discover if he were in earnest, and blurted out, "Me! My God, I never was anywhere near him!"

"I know that, Doctor," Bartley said, with a reassuring smile. "What I meant was that he was trying to point out someone; I doubt if he could distinguish one person from another. You happened to be unlucky enough to be in front of him, that is all."

"I am pretty sure he had no idea that he was pointing at me; and I doubt, for that matter, if he even knew what he was saying," Doctor Webster insisted.

"I agree with you in part, Doctor," was Bartley's answer. "I don't believe he had any idea whom he was pointing at; but I think he knew who killed him, nevertheless."

"But, Mr. Bartley," Ruth cried, wonderingly, "why should anyone wish to kill our chauffeur?"

His answer came in a short sentence. "Because he knew who killed Mr. Slyke."

His reply, not unexpected by me, seemed to surprise the others. The girl looked bewildered and Doctor King's eyes opened wide. Miss Potter alone remained unmoved. Even the district attorney, lawyer that he was, demanded, "Why do you say that?"

Bartley glanced at him as if he had expected a man with legal training to have better understanding, and in a weary voice explained, "You all recognize that Briffeur was killed as he was about to testify. Whoever did the deed was afraid of what he knew. He could not, of course, have foreseen that the lights would go out; but when they did he seized the opportunity. He feared that the chauffeur would tell who killed Slyke. And while he might not have been able to prove his statement, he knew enough to be dangerous. For myself, I believe the chauffeur could have told us, and that he was killed to shut his mouth."

The district attorney made a little gesture of dissent. "I see that; but, on the other hand, how do we know that Briffeur himself did not kill Slyke? He said, you remember, 'Slyke murdered—I—killed—' Maybe he killed him himself."

Black nodded an emphatic agreement. This accorded with the theory he had advanced the night before. I could see that Bartley, however, was not convinced. As he made no comment, the attorney continued, "He said nothing more; but may we not say that, if he had finished the sentence, what he would have said would have been, Slyke murdered. I KILLED HIM'."

"Then why was the chauffeur killed?" Bartley asked with a sarcastic smile.

The lawyer shook his head slowly, and answered that he had advanced his argument as a theory only.

"I have an idea," Bartley said, "that if the chauffeur had finished the sentence it would have been, 'Slyke murdered. I know who did it'."

As I listened to both of their theories, one seemed to me just as likely to be correct as the other.

At this point Miss Potter rose from her chair with an appealing look at Bartley, and he told her with a smile that he would not need her any longer. Accompanied by her niece, she left the room. The inquest had been a very severe strain on both of them.

When they had gone, Bartley turned to the district attorney and said gravely, "The most important statement that the chauffeur made we have not even mentioned. That is, that the two men now in prison for the robbery of a year ago, are innocent. He told us to see the boy, meaning, of course, the boy that works around the garage. Roche, you had better have someone keep an eye on him until we can talk to him."

Roche nodded and left the room.

"My reason for being here," he continued to the district attorney, "is that I came to look into that robbery."

Both the district attorney and Doctor Webster were surprised. Evidently neither of them had given a thought to what had brought him to Circle Lake.

"From what I have found out," Bartley went on, "I am of the opinion that the men now in prison are innocent. Many believe, so I am told, that the men should never have been convicted on the evidence presented. The statement that Briffeur made confirms my belief, and should free them."

The district attorney did not speak at once, when he did, he said, "I presume that the chauffeur's statement will be admitted as a dying declaration. We can make sworn affidavits as to what he said. Of course, a statement of that kind, unsupported by proof, is not enough to free them. I am not familiar with the evidence given at the trial; it took place before I went into office."

He looked at his watch, and added, "I have an appointment at five, and it's almost that now. Roche can take charge here, and Doctor King is coroner."

"Wait a minute." Bartley paused until Boche, who entered at the moment, had joined us. "There is one question I want to ask the doctors before we go. Pelt is in the chair in which Briffeur sat. Roche, you take the chair beside him, and Doctor King, you sit in the chair that Miss Potter had."

The two men did as requested, and Bartley studied them for a moment.

"Now," he said, "that is just the way the chairs were filled when the cry rang out. What I wish to know is this: do you doctors think that a person on either the right or left side of the chauffeur could have struck that blow?"

The red face of Roche flushed even redder at the suggestion in Bartley's words, but reassured by a twinkle in Bartley's eyes, he shrugged his shoulders and remarked, "It's not often a police chief is as close to a murder as I was. I'd feel more comfortable, though, if I had been sitting in the back of the room when the thing happened."

Both doctors considered Bartley's question carefully for several moments. Then Doctor Webster said, "It is physically possible for either to have stabbed him; but I don't believe either one of them did, though there is little enough to go on."

"What do you mean?" Bartley asked.

"Simply this. Take Roche, for instance. He is right handed; and, if he had stabbed him, he would have had to reach around, in a very awkward way, to make such a direct thrust, and the wound would not have been straight. The same thing applies to Miss Potter. Then, too, the blow had a great deal more force back of it than the average woman could give. I think it came from the front. Don't you, Doctor King?"

The doctor nodded agreement. Roche and he remained behind to make the necessary arrangements while the rest of us started for home.

As soon as we had passed the policemen on guard at the front door, we were surrounded by reporters, eager to discover from us just what had taken place. Bartley refused to talk and turned them over to the district attorney, who, he said, was the only one who could give out information. Many of the men who had been present at the inquest were still lingering in excited groups. They eyed us with interest as we came down the steps to the lawn, but did not attempt to approach us.

The storm had passed over and the sun was out again, bright and warm. The grass was very green and the air unusually clear and still. We looked about for Currie, who had been in the audience, but could not find him and started off without him.

Bartley did not speak until we were within sight of the house. Then he said, "I wish that the solution of Slyke's death was as easy as that of the chauffeur's."

"As easy!" I gasped.

He gave me a queer look and answered, "Yes, as easy," and added nothing more.

XI. In Which We Begin To Find A Motive

BARTLEY had some work for me to do, and I did not dine until the others had finished. While I was eating, Currie wandered into the dining room and sat down beside me. The murder had taken all the life out of him. It was the first time that he had come so close to a crime. He seemed unable to forget the cry and those awful moments in the darkened room. We discussed the affair for a while; then I excused myself and went in search of Bartley.

I found him in his room, in an easy chair, reading. The book was a little green covered thing, with the faded lettering of a bygone age. He smiled as he saw me looking at the cover, and passed me the volume. It was an old French edition of *Brantome*, the text faded by the years. I had no idea who *Brantome* was, and placed the book on the table. I wanted to talk about the murder. Bartley took out his cigar case, gave me a cigar, and lighted one for himself. We smoked in silence for a while; then he said quizzically, "Well?"

"Well, what?" I drawled back.

He watched a smoke ring curl to the ceiling. "What about this afternoon's affair?"

I had been thinking for hours of this latest crime, and no solution had come to me. I could not understand how, in those few moments of darkness, the murderer had been able to approach the chauffeur near enough to kill him, nor why the people next to him had heard nothing.

When I told Bartley of my bewilderment, he answered with a little grin, "I agree with you, Pelt, it's very mysterious. It's the first time I ever heard of murder taking place at an inquest and in a room filled with people. There are no clues, apparently. To my mind, however, the real reason for the murder was to prevent Briffeur from testifying. Whoever killed him knew about what he would say, and feared that he would tell who had killed Slyke."

"Then that means," I replied, "that Slyke's murderer must have been at the inquest."

"Of course," Bartley exclaimed in disgust. "Where do you think the murderer was? Whoever it was, had to be in the room when he killed Briffeur."

Breaking in on him, I said, "But he could not have foreseen that the lights would go out and give him a chance? I thought that it was the storm that extinguished them."

He nodded. "That's true enough. It was that last flash of lightning. Darkness was just what he needed, and he took advantage of it. He had several moments in which to act. There were not many people near enough to the chauffeur to have killed him in that short time."

He rose, went over to his bag, and brought back the knife with which the murder had been committed. For several moments he examined it, then he asked as he passed it over to me, "What do you think of it?"

It was a rather odd knife. It resembled a hunting knife, and the edge showed it had had a good deal of use. The blade was very dull except at the point. It was too large to be carried in a man's pocket, but a woman could have hidden it somewhere in the folds of her clothing.

As Bartley seemed to expect some comment from me as I handed it back to him, I said, "Save for the fact it's not very sharp and seems to have been used a great deal, I can learn nothing from it."

He smiled as he turned the knife over and over in his hand. "Oh, there's more than that. It tells a great deal. The knife is unusual in shape and length. There was a time when it was used a great deal, and the owner kept it very sharp and clean. But for some time now he has neglected it. There is one very important thing that you have overlooked. You remember those little drawings I found on the magazine in Slyke's room, the row of connected circles? I find the same thing here."

I gasped, and, reaching for the knife, looked at the wooden handle. There, faintly scratched on the wood, were a number of circles running one into the other.

"Do you think," I asked in excitement, "that it is the sign of some secret society?"

To my surprise he laughed; then looked at me to see if I were really serious, and, finding that I was, laughed again.

"No. It's simply this—that most of us, if we have a pen or pencil in our fingers, draw figures on whatever happens to be at hand. We do it without thinking, because it is a subconscious act; and, as a rule, we draw the same set of figures each time. Someone, having nothing to do, idly scratched these figures on this knife handle, hardly conscious of what he was doing. I believe the same person made the figures on the magazine and on the knife."

"Why do you think that?" I asked.

"It had been scientifically proved that, when a person plays with a pencil and idly draws figures, he always draws the same ones; and that they are symbols of something deep in his subconscious mind. These circles are so much alike that I think they were drawn by the same person."

I had a dim idea I had heard something similar to what he was saying in college, but just what it was I could not remember. As I started to hand him the knife, it slipped through my fingers and fell to the floor and stood quivering, its point imbedded in the wood. With a sudden exclamation, Bartley picked it up and, to my astonishment, let it fall again and again. Each time the point stuck upright in the floor. Then he balanced it on his hand, smiling to himself. As he replaced it in his bag, he said, "I am glad you dropped that knife, Pelt."

It seemed to me such an inane thing to say that I made no comment. ""We are going over to Slyke's again," he continued, "to see Miss Potter. By the way, there's another thing, Pelt, you can aid me a good deal by solving."

"What's that?" I said.

"Find out why that dog did not bark the night of the murder. It's a puppy, noisy and active, and does not like strangers. The person that killed Slyke, as far as we know, had to come down those long stairs and pass through the living room where the dog was. If it was someone from outside, that dog should have barked. But as far as we can find out, he never made a sound."

"It looks to me," I suggested, "as if the murder were committed by someone in the house."

Bartley did not answer until he had opened the door into the hall, then he paused to say, "There seems to be no motive for any of the family to have killed Slyke. The little difficulty between Miss Potter and Slyke does not seem important enough to consider. The will has been found and all the property is accounted for. His lawyer, you remember, discovered a large sum of money in the safe when it was opened." Then he proceeded downstairs.

It was only a short drive in Bartley's fast car to the Slyke house. He offered no explanation of our call, and I hid my curiosity as well as I could.

The butler took our hats and ushered us into a small room at the end of the long living room. The walls were lined with sectional book cases, filled with sets of the cheap subscription books that everybody buys and nobody reads, and in the center of the room was a library table covered with magazines. In a nearby chair Miss Potter was seated with an Ouija board on a stand beside her. She rose at our entrance, and motioned to us to be seated, then sat down again. The ordeal of the last few days, especially the shock of having the chauffeur killed at her side, had unnerved her. Her hands trembled, and she forced a smile with difficulty.

As soon as the butler had gone, Bartley came at once to the object of his visit.

"Miss Potter," he said, "the butler testified this afternoon that he overheard words between Mr. Slyke and yourself. Would you mind telling me what they were?"

Her face flushed, but she kept her eyes on Bartley as she replied coldly, "The butler was mistaken. Mr. Slyke and myself never quarrelled."

"Oh, I don't mean that you actually quarrelled, but that you had some words."

Her eyes dropped under his searching gaze, and it was not until he had repeated his question a second time that she answered rather reluctantly, "There was no—no trouble. What the butler spoke of had nothing to do with Mr. Slyke's death."

Bartley noticed her hesitation, and asked suddenly, "Was it over his selling whiskey?"

She started and her face paled, then flushed. In a low voice she demanded, "How did you know?"

"That is not of much importance, is it? I am right; that was what the words were about, wasn't it?"

She gave him an appealing look, then glanced back at the floor. At last she regained her composure, and, raising her eyes, answered, "Yes. That was what the butler heard us talking about. It was not a quarrel. I told him he would get into trouble over the whiskey, and he told me it was none of my business."

"When did he start to sell it?"

She thought for a moment. "I am not sure. You see, I know very little about it. But before the prohibition law came into effect he bought a great quantity of whiskey. He told me that a man who had whiskey could make a lot of money. He got several truck loads, but where he kept it I don't know."

"And after prohibition, did he buy any more?" Bartley asked.

"I think so. I think it came from Canada. He told me once or twice that he was making a great deal of money out of it."

"And you quarrelled over his selling it?"

Rather warmly she answered, "We never quarrelled. It was not my affair. I felt badly, of course, that he should do a thing like that. I warned him that he would get into trouble, and he told me it was none of my business if he did. That must have been what the butler heard."

Bartley glanced sharply at her. "Have you any idea who helped him in it?"

"No—that is—I never knew. I did think that maybe—"

She stopped and Bartley suggested, "You thought it was the chauffeur?"

"Yes, I did. I know that Mr. Slyke bought a truck, and that the chauffeur would have long talks with him in his room, and then take the truck and be away for several days. In the last year or so, he became overbearing, and I wondered why Mr. Slyke kept him—unless there was something between them."

I was not surprised. Everything had seemed to lead up to this revelation. What I could not understand was why a man in Mr. Slyke's position should be engaged in the illegal selling of whiskey, and take his chauffeur into his confidence. Whiskey bought in any quantity, since prohibition, had to come from Canada, and passed through the hands of a number of men. Was his engaging in selling whiskey a problem in itself, or had it some bearing on his death?

Miss Potter had little more to tell us, and we rose to take our leave. As Bartley took his hat, he asked her if she had been using the Ouija board.

She was at once excited, her eyes gleamed, and her voice rose as she responded, "Yes, I received a message from Mr. Slyke. I know it was from him. He has written twice, 'You will hear from me,' and 'I know I will'. I am going to get a good medium to come and see what he wants to communicate to me."

To my surprise Bartley listened gravely, almost reverently. When she had finished, he said he knew of a very good medium and would try to arrange for him to come to the house for a séance if she desired. This proposal pleased Miss Potter very much, and she accepted at once. She told us that many people in Saratoga believed in spiritualism, including Doctor King. For a while they discussed various manifestations; and I listened to Bartley in astonishment, as he told of receiving messages from the dead, for I knew he did not believe in them.

We were interrupted by a knock, and the butler entered with a telegram for Bartley. It had been sent first to Currie's, and he had directed the boy to follow us to Slyke's.

Bartley tore open the envelope and ran his eyes over the paper. I saw him start, then without a word he handed it to me, and I read:

"Arrested in New York one o'clock this morning Jacob Asher with truck load of whiskey. Claims he paid Slyke $23,000 for it afternoon before his death. Saw him about five o'clock. Did not know Slyke was dead till he read papers. Story seems to be true.
Rogers "

No wonder Bartley had started. Here at last might be a motive for the murder. Perhaps the man in New York could tell us what had happened that night.

With grave face Bartley took the telegram from my hand, and reread it; then he asked Miss Potter if Slyke had had a visitor the afternoon before his death. She said she did not know whether he had or not, as he had been away most of the afternoon. After a few more questions, we bade her good night. In the doorway Bartley paused to say something to her, in so low a tone that I could not catch his words; but I did hear her eager answering "Yes."

As we climbed into the car and started down the road, I said that I did not suppose she knew anything about the $23,000 whiskey deal. His answer was as quick as a flash, "I never thought she did. The strange thing is that

in the safe, after his death, his lawyer should find
$10,000, and that he should have made a deposit of
$13,000 that same afternoon."

We rode in silence for a while. Then he startled me by
saying that he was not going back to Currie's, but to New
York to interview the man arrested with the whiskey,
and that he would not be back until the next afternoon. It
was not until we were at the station, waiting for his train,
that I interrupted his preoccupation to ask if he thought
it would ever be discovered who had killed Briffeur.

The flickering lights above us cast weird shadows over
his face, and it seemed to me that behind his half smile
was a look of great sadness as he replied, "I know now
who killed Briffeur."

"You do?" I gasped.

He answered slowly, "Yes. That was easy enough to
discover. But to prove it before a jury will be almost
impossible."

Just then the train came in and he said no more. On
my way back to the house I pondered deeply over his last
remark, but could find no clue to his meaning.

XII. In Which The Robbery Is Solved

I HAD intended to spend the next morning in either fishing or playing golf. Bartley had left in such a hurry that he had given me no instructions as to what I was to do in his absence. But when I came down to breakfast, by my plate was a telegram from him, reminding me to see the boy in the garage and learn from him what he knew of the robbery. I had entirely forgotten the chauffeur's dying statement.

After a late breakfast, I took the car and drove once more to the Slyke house. As I went along, I speculated upon what that boy could know. The day I had seen him in Slyke's living room, he had impressed me as being an average country boy without much education, who did odd jobs around a garage. It seemed almost impossible that he should know anything of value about the robbery that had taken place the year before; yet the chauffeur, just before he had died, had said that the boy could explain the mystery.

Leaving the car in the driveway in front of the house, I went around to the rear. The house appeared deserted, although it was the day of Slyke's funeral.

The garage was some yards from the house, half hidden among the trees. It was two stories high, built of stone, the upper story being used as living quarters for the men employed in it. The door stood open and I entered. Coming from the bright sunlight into the darkened room, it was several moments before I could see clearly enough to make out that it was occupied by a large touring car, two small runabouts, and a large truck. There was no one in sight, and after waiting a moment, I called loudly. The boy I wished to see, slouched out from a back room.

He was about eighteen, with heavy figure, red face and unbrushed hair. His suit was dirty with oil from the cars. If he wondered what I wanted, he gave no sign of it. His eyes met mine clearly and honestly, as if he had no secrets to hide.

As I knew our talk would take some time, I climbed into the front seat of the touring car and motioned him to take a place beside me. I told him what the chauffeur had said before he died. It was clear that no one had mentioned it to him, for his mouth dropped open in astonishment and he seemed dazed. He had known, of course, that the chauffeur had been murdered; but he had not known that he had involved him in his dying statement.

At first he stoutly denied that he knew anything at all about the robbery. He seemed to have the idea that I thought he was implicated in it. All he admitted knowing, was a bit of gossip that he had picked up around the house at the time it was committed. The more I questioned him, the more he insisted that he knew nothing about it, and I almost believed him. But the chauffeur, at the point of death, had said, "Ask the boy." It stood to reason then that he must know something of importance. At last I told him that the chauffeur had insisted that he knew, and asked if anyone had ever told him anything about the crime. A startled look came into his face; and he turned to me excitedly, his words tumbling over each other.

"Maybe that's what he meant. But, good Lord, I thought it was a joke, darned if I didn't. I thought he was kidding me; he was drunk, you know."

"Who was drunk?" I asked.

"Briffeur. He was very drunk, sir. You see, you asked me did I know anything about those men breaking into Slyke's, and I didn't; but Briffeur told me one night—"

He paused.

"Go on," I commanded.

"It was one night soon after the trial. Briffeur came drifting in here, pretty well lighted up. When he was that way, he used to talk a lot; but he never told the truth at such times, as I'd often found out. He never knew afterwards what he had been saying. He would tell awful yarns about women, and the like. No one ever believed him."

I brought the boy to the point by asking what it was the chauffeur had told him. He hesitated, then in a voice that showed that he thought what he was going to say was almost too foolish to mention, he added, "He got to talking about that robbery, and said it was to laugh, the way the trial had gone. That no one knew that he had committed the robbery—no one except himself and one other. I thought, of course, it was one of his wild yarns, and laughed at him. When I asked him why he did it, he said Slyke owed him lots of money, and that he was after it."

It was natural that the boy should have thought this conversation of no more importance than many others of the chauffeur, when he was drunk and boasting about things that had never happened. He had laughed at the story and thought no more of it. To him, the fact that the men were convicted proved their guilt. I realized that the chauffeur, his tongue loosened by liquor, had told the truth for once, and that the mystery of the robbery was solved. I asked the boy to tell me in detail just what had happened.

The chauffeur, he said, had come into the garage, "lit up like a battleship." The talk had veered around to the robbery, and he had boasted that the two men were in jail for the robbery that he himself had committed. "Who had helped him, he did not say. He claimed that Slyke owed him "lots of money." It seemed absurd that a wealthy man like Slyke should owe his chauffeur money and not pay it. He had even boasted that the evidence against the men in prison was arranged by himself.

It seems that the morning after the robbery he had gone to the post office for the mail, and a copy of the "Boston Evening Times," a paper to which Slyke did not subscribe, had been handed to him by mistake. He had been reading a book only a few days before, "filled with murders and the like," and he remembered the account of a robbery in it and how the evidence was manufactured. On his way home, he stopped at the police station for information, and offered to drive the police out to the home of the men who had been arrested. It seems that the state police had taken them to their own homes and allowed one of the men to change his coat before taking him to jail. The local police wanted to search the coat which had been left behind. It was here that the chauffeur had his first idea of planting the evidence. He tore the corner off the paper, and at the man's house managed to slip the newspaper into the pocket of the coat before the police examined it. Later, at Slyke's, he threw the little torn piece of paper on the floor so that they could find that, too.

The boy said that Briffeur had told the story with great gusts of laughter and much swearing. His manner was so much that of one telling a story to impress an ignorant boy, that the boy had not believed for a second that he was serious. The next morning, when he had spoken to the chauffeur about it, he had replied with a great laugh, "I did pull your leg, didn't I. It was easy enough to see why a simple country boy had attached no importance to the story, and believed it only a drunken man's foolish yarn.

When he had finished, I wondered if the boy had not been right when he thought that the man had been simply fooling him. But if it were true, his story, taken with the dying words of the chauffeur, would be enough to free the men in prison. I decided to take him with me to the police station and let him tell his story to Roche.

On our arrival in Saratoga, we were lucky enough to find both Roche and Black together. Without any comment on my part, I had the boy repeat his story to the two officers. They listened with a good deal of interest. Roche, of course, had handled the robbery, and knew more about it than Black; but Black, I knew, believed that Briffeur was the murderer of Slyke, and the boy's story confirmed his belief.

Roche, his big face beaming with interest, listened until the boy had finished; then he sent him into another room and, turning to us, exclaimed, "That's the darndest story I ever heard."

We debated the story for an hour, Roche taking the view that the chauffeur might have been fooling the boy, and Black that the chauffeur had told the truth and was too drunk to realize what he had said.

Roche clinched his argument by demanding, "Why, under heaven, should Slyke owe Briffeur a large sum of money?"

That was, we all agreed, the weak point in the story.

"My Lord," Roche exclaimed as a thought occurred to him, "do you realize that it was Briffeur that found the torn piece of cloth on the rose bush, the piece that fitted into the man's pants?"

In astonishment I asked, "It was?"

"It sure was. He came into the police station a few days later with it and told us where he had discovered it, and asked if we knew what it was. We found later that it fitted into a hole in the pants one of the fellows was wearing."

"Was he ever in the cell with those men?" Black asked, with a glance at me.

"Yes, several times. Slyke asked that we let him go in and talk to them."

Black threw out his hands in disgust. "My God, Roche, one would think you kept a hotel. You let anyone go in and out that wanted to."

Roche flushed, and replied angrily, "Well, Slyke had lots of pull here, and I don't think it did any harm to let his chauffeur see those men."

"None," said Black drily. "It only gave him a chance to snip a piece from one of the men's trousers."

'That's foolish," Roche laughed.

"Oh, I don't know," was Black's answer. "You can't prove he did not. You never saw the piece of cloth until he brought it in to you. He was in the cell alone with them, and had the chance to cut out the piece of cloth. You can't prove that the chauffeur's story is not true. It fits in better with facts than the evidence that sent those men to jail. But, oh boy, the easy way you run this jail!"

Roche scowled at us, and was about to retort when he was called from the room. Black and I lighted cigars and smoked in silence.

"Mr. Pelt," he asked at last, "what do you think of my theory that Briffeur murdered Slyke?"

I had given little thought to the matter, and said as much. Black surprised me by adding, "You know that Doctor King and the district attorney think that the only verdict that can be brought in in the Slyke case, is suicide?"

"They do?" I asked in astonishment.

He nodded. "Yes, they do. They seem to think that the evidence is so very slight that it will be impossible to prove it was not suicide. It is usual to bring in a verdict of suicide in cases like this. The fact that Miss Potter testified that she closed his eyes, leads to the possibility that she might have pulled the bed clothes up around his neck also. They don't seem to think that Mr. Bartley's talk about the way the fingers clasped the gun, and the way his arms were arranged inside the bed clothes, are enough evidence for a verdict of murder. I myself, though, believe that he was murdered."

Black's remarks astonished me. True, I realized that it was almost impossible to present convincing legal proof that Slyke had been murdered, but there was still the chauffeur's death to be explained. If he had been killed, as Bartley thought, because he knew too much about Slyke's death, then it seemed to me that to bring in a verdict of suicide would be impossible. I told Black of this objection, and he agreed with me.

Then he reiterated his belief in Briffeur's guilt. According to him, the story the chauffeur told the boy fitted in well with his own theory. True, there was little to base it on, so far as evidence went; but, assuming that Slyke and the chauffeur had quarrelled about money, his strongest bit of evidence was Briffeur's coming to the vault where the missing revolver was hidden. No one else, so far as we knew, had quarrelled with Slyke, or had any reason for wanting to kill him. Black explained the chauffeur's death by saying Miss Potter had killed him. I told him this last disproved his first theory, that whoever had killed the chauffeur, had done so because he knew too much. about Slyke's death.

I found that it was nearly four o'clock, and as I had had no luncheon I decided to get something to eat before Bartley's train came in. Just as I reached the door, Black called after me, "Say, Pelt, what does your chief want us all over for, to Slyke's tonight?"

This was the first time that I had heard we were expected to go there; and, seeing my astonishment, he added that Bartley had sent word for Roche and himself to be at Slyke's promptly at eight o'clock. I was forced to admit that I did not know as much about it as he did.

I went to a little tea room on the main street, and had almost finished my meal when some one called my name, and a reporter from the "Record," whom I knew, rose and joined me. He mentioned the Slyke case and said that everyone was waiting for Bartley to "spring something." He complained that there was little enough information to be gotten about it. All he had been able to do had been to interview the men that had been at Slyke's home the night of his death. One of them told him, however, that three or four times during the evening Slyke had tried to reach someone on the 'phone—just who, he did not know.

I had now barely time to reach the station before Bartley's train pulled in, and I bade him a hurried farewell.

As Bartley and I drove down the main street of Saratoga, he said, "By the way, Pelt, stop at a store and get me five slates."

"Five what?" I asked.

He grinned. "Five slates. The kind used years ago in school. I want them all the same size."

"But," I gasped, "what do you want with five slates?"

He threw back his head and laughed. "They are usually used to write on, Pelt, but you will find out tonight what I want them for."

I stopped at a little stationery store, and returned in a moment with five slates. As I was getting back into the car, I remembered what the reporter had told me about Slyke's trying to get someone on the telephone, and I repeated his story to Bartley. He said nothing for a moment, then asked me to drive to the telephone exchange. He spent ten minutes in the building; and, when he came out, he seemed well pleased with his visit but did not mention its result.

As we drove along, I told him the boy's story. When I had finished he smiled. "I believe the chauffeur told the boy the truth. He had been drinking, but that is when a man often speaks the truth."

I glanced at him to see if he were in earnest, and he nodded. "Yes, I am serious. Briffeur had broken into Slyke's house. He never spoke of this crime, but he thought a good deal about it. When he got drunk, his subconscious mind told the secret that he was trying to hide. I believe that what Briffeur said was the truth about the robbery."

"But why should he try to rob Slyke?" I asked.

"I am not sure. My theories are beginning to make a more or less connected whole, but there are still some gaps to be bridged."

We were almost on Currie's driveway before I remembered to mention what Black had said about the probability of a verdict of suicide being brought in.

"Then the verdict has not been given yet?" Bartley asked.

I shook my head.

"I can see, Pelt, that suicide seems the only possible verdict to them. But I think we can aid them in forming another."

Currie heard the car as it stopped before the house and came out to greet Bartley. As Mrs. Currie was in town, we did not change for dinner. During the meal the murder was not mentioned. Bartley went to his room immediately afterward. I sat with Currie for a while, smoking; then I excused myself. I was eager to learn what Bartley had discovered in New York. I found him in his room, stretched out in a big armchair, one leg thrown over its arm, his pipe in his mouth. As I watched him I thought how little one would suppose that he was engaged in solving two mystifying murders. He looked up as I entered, smiled, and went back to his reading.

"How did your trip come off?" I asked.

"Well, Pelt," he drawled, as he placed his long yellow covered book on the floor, "Arentino certainly knew the criminal life of his day."

His remark had, of course, to do with the book that he had been reading, and nothing with my question. Seeing my disappointment, he laughed. "The trip wasn't of much importance. The man did buy the whiskey from Slyke. He had bought all that was in the vault, but had only removed one truck load when he was caught. He paid $23,000 for it that afternoon, and left on the seven o'clock train for New York. His alibi is perfect; he knows nothing about the murder. The alibi of the men on the truck also is perfect. They did not reach Saratoga until noon on the day after Slyke's death. They dealt only with one man."

"One man?" I echoed. "Who?"

He watched my face for a moment, then replied simply, "Briffeur!"

I had half expected that answer. It made the chauffeur's story that Slyke owed him money seem reasonable. It even hinted that the chauffeur had tried to blackmail Slyke, and made Black's theory that Briffeur had killed Slyke seem not unreasonable.

"The men on the truck," Bartley continued, "did not know Briffeur's name; but their description of the man who unlocked the door of the vault for them fitted Briffeur."

"But—" I ventured.

"But what?" he countered.

"That connects Slyke and Briffeur."

He was silent for a moment, his face grave. Then he said slowly, "Yes, Pelt, it does. If the chauffeur had not been killed himself, he would be suspected of causing Slyke's death. But there is one thing—"

"And what is that?" I asked eagerly.

"Briffeur said someone else was implicated in that robbery. What I want to know is, who was that other man?" He paused, then added, "There is no doubt, Pelt, that Slyke had been selling whiskey for some time. Where he got it, and who was in on it with him, we don't know. Maybe tonight we can find out."

Currie's voice called from below that the car was waiting to take us to Slyke's house, and we rose. As I started for the door, Bartley handed me a package and gave me a playful shove.

"Don't drop them," he laughed.

I gave him a disgusted look. "But these are the slates."

"So they are, but they may talk for us tonight."

And with that absurd suggestion in my ears, I went down the stairs to join Currie.

XIII. OUT OF THE DARKNESS

I WONDERED as we drove along the country road what was the reason for our visit. The funeral had been held that afternoon, and it did not seem a suitable time for callers. Currie was as much in the dark as I as to Bartley's reason for choosing this particular time.

Roche and Black were waiting for us on the front steps; and I could tell from their excited manner that they, too, considered this no ordinary visit. Bartley's manner, also, was much like that I had seen him have when he was about to reach the solution of one of his most baffling cases; yet as far as I could see, we were no nearer a solution than on the first day. Even Currie noticed that something was wrong, and I caught him stealing puzzled glances at his friend. Roche and Black, after a few short words of greeting, lapsed into silence.

The butler seemed to expect us, and showed us at once into the large room in which the inquest had been held. Bartley placed his bag and the package of slates on a small table in the center of the room, Roche sat down heavily in a chair, and the rest of us stood until Miss Potter entered. She seemed to be expecting us also, and for the first time, since I had met her, seemed almost at her ease. As she greeted us the bell rang, and a moment later the butler ushered in Doctor King. He glanced at Bartley, then gave us all a word of greeting.

We seated ourselves around the table with the exception of Bartley, who remained standing at one end. He was a different Bartley from the one who had laughed and joked with us during the past few days. His face was stern, and his tired eyes glanced from one to the other of us soberly. The butler brought in a glass of water and placed it on the table.

Bartley waited until he had left the room again before he spoke, his voice low and hesitating:

"I have brought you here tonight at Miss Potter's request. She believes that it is possible to get in touch with the spirits of the dead, and that we may receive a message from Mr. Slyke that will tell us who killed him. She has asked us to be present as witnesses."

Currie looked at me as if he thought that Bartley had gone crazy. I was too surprised to offer an excuse. A glance at Bartley showed that he was in earnest, and I sank back in my chair bewildered. I knew that he did not believe in spiritualism, though he was familiar with the question from all sides and had made a special study of it. I was puzzled as to why he should stoop to this pretense. Doctor King seemed more surprised than any of us; after a startled look at Bartley, he shrugged his shoulders and whispered something to Roche, who in turn shook his head.

"While I was in New York," Bartley continued, "I arranged for a certain medium, who is claimed to have had wonderful results, to meet us here tonight. I did not tell him what we expected, or anything about the circumstances. He will be here in a few moments. Meanwhile I am going to try a little experiment of my own."

He paused, then continued, "You know it is believed by thousands, that messages from the spirit world are written on slates by unseen hands. The test of the genuineness of such messages is the absence of an opportunity for fraud on the part of the medium, and the fact that it is in the handwriting of the person who is believed to be sending them. If these tests are met, we can then assume that the message was not the work of the medium, but comes from outside sources. I have a number of slates here, and am going to try to secure a message on them. I am not sure if I can do it, however."

Currie interrupted to say, "But, John, if the lights are turned out, how are we to know that you did not write those messages yourself?"

Without a smile on his face Bartley replied, "I did not intend to turn out the light. I am going to do what few mediums ever attempt to do: that is, to see if we can secure a message on these slates in full light. There have been so many frauds in slate writing séances that a test made in the dark has no value."

As he spoke, he tore the wrapping from the package and disclosed a number of ordinary school slates tied together with a string. When he had cut the string and placed the slates on the table before him, he added, "You might claim that these slates already have a message written on them, so I will wash the surface of each with water. If there was any writing on them, it will be wiped out."

With our eyes following every moment, he took a piece of cloth, dipped it into the glass of water, and carefully washed one side of a slate. As he was beginning to wash the other side, he paused and said to Currie, "You may think I have not washed the slate thoroughly enough; suppose, Currie, you take it and wash the other side yourself. Make a good job of it."

Currie's eagerness was almost laughable as he took the slate and turned it over and over, examining both surfaces. Then he thoroughly washed it. When he had finished he whispered to me, "There was not a darned thing on that slate."

The same method was employed with the other slates. First, Bartley would wash one side, then would call upon one of us to examine the slate and wash off the other side. I was left until the last, and I examined my slate very carefully before I touched it with the cloth. On the side which Bartley had washed little drops of water still clung. The unwashed side was dirty but showed no traces of having been written on.

When I had finished my task, Bartley took one of the slates and said, "You have seen there was no writing of any kind on these slates. I am going to give one to each of you. Miss Potter should place hers under her feet; Currie might sit on his; the rest of you can place them under your coats."

He gave us each a slate, and we did as he suggested. I wondered, as I placed mine under my coat, just what Bartley expected to discover. Somehow the whole thing seemed so absurd. He was so serious about it, however, that I began to believe that he must expect to receive a message of some sort. We sat silent and expectant, I, for one, feeling a little foolish.

Bartley, who had glanced at his watch several times, waited for five minutes to pass before he said, "Suppose, Currie, you look at your slate."

Currie grinned, as if to say he considered it all foolishness, but did as requested. As he glanced at his slate, the smile left his face, his jaw dropped, and his eyes grew big with wonder. He looked at it several seconds as if he could not believe his eyes, then slowly passed it to me. I took it eagerly, glanced at it, and in my turn was startled. There, in a sprawling hand, running across the slate that had been blank a few moments before, was written, "Currie, people who steal whiskey out of a vault at midnight will come to a bad end."

Almost unable to credit my eyes, I stared at the slate. Both sides had been so thoroughly washed that when Currie had taken it they were still wet. How the writing had gotten on the slate, I could not imagine.

I snatched my slate from under my coat. There was something on it, too—the sketch of a revolver—and under it, in a handwriting that was the same as that on Currie's slate, the single word "murder" had been written. Five minutes before, the slate had been absolutely blank!

Miss Potter gave a sudden cry. She had risen to her feet with shining eyes. Holding her slate in one trembling hand, she tried to speak, failed, then cried triumphantly,

"It's a message—a message—from Mr. Slyke! I knew it would come," and sank back into her chair, adding, as if unable to believe the evidence of her own senses, "It's in his own handwriting, his very own, and he tells me what to do."

Bartley took the slate from her trembling fingers, a curious expression on his face. He placed it on the table, and we crowded round to examine it. This time the entire surface of the slate was covered with writing, in the same sprawling hand that had written on Currie's and mine. The letters were large and looked as if the person who had written the message had been very weak. Too astonished to speak, we bent and read:

"All will be well with me if you aid those who are trying to discover who injured me. For my peace, do this: listen to the medium—" and the message trailed off in a large S.

"It's Mr. Slyke's writing," Miss Potter cried excitedly. "I recognize it. There was nothing on the slate when I placed my feet on it."

Bartley faced her gravely, with something in his manner that gave me the impression that he was not at all surprised at what was happening.

"Then you are absolutely sure it is in his writing?" he asked.

Not trusting herself to speak, she simply nodded.

At that moment the bell rang, and the butler passed through the room on his way to the door. In the second before his return, I saw Doctor King steal a look at his slate, and, from the startled look on his face, I knew that he, too, had received a message. Meeting my eyes, he gave me a faint, wondering smile and shook his head doubtfully.

The man whom the butler ushered in, was the medium that Bartley had secured in New York. He was very tall and thin, dressed in black, with white, unhealthy face, shifty eyes, and hair a bit too long.

After he had been introduced, Bartley told us that we were to begin the séance at once. The first thing to be done, was to place the medium in a chair in the corner and tie his hands and feet firmly. Roche was selected to draw the rope through the rungs of the chair, tie his hands behind his back, and place a gag in his mouth so that he could not speak. He performed his task with the thoroughness of a police officer trained in the work; and when he informed us that the medium could neither move nor speak, I believed him.

At Bartley's suggestion we seated ourselves around the table. It was a small one, not very heavy in construction. We placed our hands on its surface as directed, and linked them together by hooking the thumb and little finger of each hand around the finger of the hand next to it. We were told that under no circumstance were we to break this circle.

Bartley spent some time in making sure that we were arranged in the proper manner. I was seated with Currie on my left, my little finger clasped around his thumb, and Bartley himself on my right. He rose and turned off the lights, then groped his way back to my side, and a second later his finger closed around mine.

I confess that I felt a bit like a fool as I waited there in the pitch darkness. What we were doing seemed childish; yet, back of it all, there was such a general air of expectancy that I was tense with excitement. The great draperies had been drawn over the windows, and not even a ray of light penetrated the room. Just what it was that we were waiting for, I did not know. Something might or might not take place, the medium had said. We sat in silence for a number of minutes, minutes that dragged endlessly. I must confess that to me they were not the most pleasant I had ever spent.

Someone drew a deep breath, and I thought the table had started to move. Then a silence followed, so deep that I could not hear even my neighbor breathing. I felt as if I were all alone in the darkness. Only the reassuring touch of the fingers on each side of me drew me back to sanity.

Suddenly, when I was least expecting it, I felt the table under my fingers sway back and forth for a second, then fall back upon the floor with a little bang. Currie breathed hard, as if afraid; and his grasp on my fingers tightened. Then without warning, came a series of ten knocks, faintly, as if someone were knocking at a distant door. I could not tell where they came from. They seemed to be in the air, on the floor, everywhere but on the table. One thing was sure; they did not come from the direction in which the medium sat. Beside, he had been tied too tightly in his chair to have been able to make them.

Silence again, then more raps, quick little running raps, never very loud, that would start and stop a second, then trip away like little feet running to and fro.

"Are you there?" Bartley's voice asked, hesitatingly.

Almost before his words had died away, there came a series of loud raps, almost falling over each other.

Then Bartley's voice again, cool but low, "Can you communicate with us?"

I had expected that the raps would reply at once, but instead there was a long silence. Several times Bartley repeated the question, and still no answer.

At length he asked, "Shall we try some other method?"

Raps answered, tumbling over each other in their eagerness, and the table tipped so violently that I expected it would fall over. It returned to an upright position with a bang, then silence again. A deep moan from the direction of the medium startled me, then more moans interspersed with sighs.

A shrill, thin voice, ghostly and far away, said brokenly, "Oh—o oh—I—ff feel you; I know—you are— there—there—"

A silence, in which I hardly dared to breathe. The table tipped a second time and a deep voice which seemed familiar, though I could not place it, said, "I am here—

here, though you do—not see—me. I was murdered by—by—"

What it might have added we never knew. Miss Potter suddenly cried out, not in fear but in joy, "It's Mr. Slyke—his voice—"

Bartley, afraid that she might rise in her excitement and break the circle, whispered to her, and she settled back.

I now recognized the voice as that of Slyke, a little changed, it is true, but enough like it to be easily identified. I was too dazed to think; the raps, the darkness, the voice, and the fear that was creeping into my heart, were almost more than I could bear.

Silence again, broken only by the uneasy moans of the medium. Then, without warning, someone cried in terror, "Look! The stairs, the stairs!"

Almost in front of us was the stairway leading to the tower room. There, upon the top step, was a tiny light, unlike any light that I had ever seen. It was hardly larger than a silver dollar, of an unearthly whiteness; then it began to grow larger and larger, until it changed into a luminous arm floating in the air. I heard someone gasp in fear, then all was silence again. The light continued to change. Now there were two arms, then the trunk of a body, and then, out of nothing, an entire human figure appeared, glowing with a soft pale light in the darkness. A misty figure with ghostly, shining feet and hands, but no head! It began to float down the stairs, a step at a time, seemingly upon the air.

Currie's hand trembled under mine; and I controlled my own fear with an effort, as I pressed it reassuringly.

Half way down the stairs a head appeared above the body. One moment there was nothing there; the next, a face with burning eyes and tangled hair. I knew instinctively whose it was. It belonged to Slyke, the murdered man. A voice that seemed to come from the mouth said, "I have come back to place my hand on the person that killed me."

The figure took a step toward us, the table before us fell over on the floor with a crash, and a voice almost at my elbow cried in terror, "For God's sake, turn on that light. Don't let that damned thing touch me."

As suddenly as it had appeared, the figure vanished, and we were left in the darkness.

XIV: The Murderer Speaks

WHO turned on the lights I do not know. As soon as they flashed on, we looked at each other inquiringly, our eyes filled with fear. Who had cried out in terror and broken the circle? Currie's face was white and he was wiping the sweat from his brow. Miss Potter was exultant, like a person that had received a revelation. The doctor's face was very white and Roche was too frightened even to move; Black was staring blankly at Bartley, the only self possessed person in the room. With an amused little smile playing around his lips, he released the medium who was still bound and gagged in his chair. His face was pale, and when he was freed, he rubbed his arms and legs vigorously to restore their circulation. After a short whispered word with Bartley, he left the room; and a moment later we heard the front door close behind him.

What was expected of us next? It seemed to me that we had gone through enough for one night. I could find no explanation for what had taken place; I had seen with my own eyes the figure of Slyke, and heard the cry of terror from the lips of the murderer. But whose? It seemed to have all resulted in so little.

Bartley motioned us to sit down again, and took his stand back of the table. He seemed to me to be very weary, and his eyes rested on us sadly, as if he were reluctant to proceed further. It was not until we moved restlessly under his intent gaze that he said, "I am not going to make any comment on what we have just seen." He paused for a second, then added impressively, "But I think I ought to tell you that I know who killed both Slyke and Briffeur."

There was a murmur of astonishment. Currie looked
at me appealingly, but I knew no more than he. Roche
whispered to Black, and they exchanged looks of
bewilderment.

Bartley still hesitated, as if he were very; reluctant to
continue.

"I know that some of you doubt if we can prove that
Mr. Slyke was murdered. You say there are no clues, and
I admit that I have never seen a case in which there were
so few. There is no doubt, however, that he was
murdered, though it is difficult to say what the motive
was. In the case of Briffeur, it was very simple."

"Simple!" Roche gasped.

"Yes, simple. There was but one reason and one way,
and even one person that could have killed him."

This statement was too much for Roche; he shook his
head in disbelief.

"Let's consider Mr. Slyke's death for a moment,"
Bartley continued. "After the party was over, Slyke asked
Mr. Lawrence to stay behind and offered to sell him some
whiskey. They had a drink, then Lawrence went home.
But we found three glasses on the table the next morning,
showing that someone else beside Lawrence had drunk
with Slyke. Let us say this third person killed Slyke.
Understand me; I do not believe that, when he came, he
had any intention of killing him—that came later. We
will assume that Slyke and this third person went up on
the balcony, for what reason I cannot say, but I am sure
that Slyke was the one that suggested going there. No
murderer would have selected it, voluntarily, as a place
in which to kill his victim."

He paused for a second, then continued, "After Slyke
had been killed, the thought occurred to the murderer
that it was possible to make his death look like suicide.
He undressed the body in the room above the bed room,
and later carried his clothing downstairs, placing it on a
chair beside the bed. But he overlooked a stocking that
had fallen on the floor behind the door of the room above.

Criminals, no matter how shrewd, always make some mistake that betrays them; this person drew the bed clothes up around Slyke's neck. If he had not done that, I doubt if we would ever have suspected that Slyke was murdered. The shot took effect at once. It would have been impossible for him to have drawn the bed clothes up around his own neck, and placed his hands by his side before he died."

The doctor's voice sounded perplexed as he said, "But, Mr. Bartley, this is all a rather fine spun theory."

Roche murmured his agreement with the doctor's objection.

"I expected that someone would say that," Bartley smiled. "It is more than an unsupported theory. However, let us proceed. The murderer went down to the living room and brought back with him two cards, which he threw on the floor of the room where the glasses were. If its being suicide was questioned, then the finding of the cards would throw suspicion on the members of the card party."

"He was a pretty cool hand," Black interrupted.

"Yes, he was cool enough. He went downstairs into the room where the dog was—"

"But—" Roche commenced.

Bartley did not let him finish. "Yes, I know. The dog should have barked. The reason he did not was because the man was no stranger to him."

The doctor spoke once more, "But you have not proved any of these things are so; you are just supposing."

"No," came the answer, "I have not, but let us consider some of the points that have been proved. Slyke tried to telephone several times during the evening and failed to get his party each time."

Roche and Black were astonished. This was the first time they had heard anything about the telephone calls.

"When he failed again and again to get the person he wanted," Bartley continued, "he asked central to try and locate him for him. All calls from here go through the

Saratoga exchange, and it was very easy to find out whom he wanted. But that is not all. On a magazine found on the table beside the whiskey glasses were a number of little circles drawn with a pencil, circles that ran into each other."

"What has that to do with it?" asked Black, voicing his wonder.

"A great deal. Those same circles were on the handle of the knife with which Briffeur was killed. I have also a little piece of paper with similar circles drawn on it, and I know the person who drew them. It has been proved scientifically that if a person is playing with a pencil and begins to make figures unthinkingly on anything, his subconscious mind will trick him into always drawing the same design. I found the circles on the magazine in Slyke's room, on the knife that killed Briffeur, and again on the piece of paper. I know to whom Slyke telephoned, and I know also a person who saw the murderer enter the house to call on Slyke the night he was killed."

We leaned forward breathlessly to catch his words, which came with a cold, cutting edge, as he added crisply, "Now, knowing all this, don't you think that the person that drew the circles, that was telephoned to, that was seen going into Slyke's, has something to explain? Don't you think so, Doctor King?"

There was no answer, and Bartley demanded sternly, "Doctor King, you are not going to deny, are you, that you killed those two men?"

The question was so unexpected that I sat stunned. He was the last man I should have suspected. Currie cried, "My God, John," and fell silent. The doctor's face had gone a dead white, and he sank limply back in his chair. Without raising his eyes, he stammered, scarcely above a whisper, the words drawn from him against his will, "Noo—no—I killed them both."

The next instant he realized what he had said and half rose from his chair, then fell back, clasping his head in his hands. I could not believe my ears. That Bartley should suspect the doctor of the murders seemed incredible enough; but that the doctor himself should admit that it was true was beyond belief.

Roche looked first at the doctor, then at Bartley, his eyes bulging with astonishment. Black alone seemed to realize all that the doctor's admission entailed. Currie was still too dazed to understand, for King had been a good friend of his. Bartley broke the silence with, "We have proved that the doctor is the guilty party. He himself has admitted it. I have suspected him for some time, but when he gave that cry as Slyke's figure appeared, I knew that I was right."

The doctor was still sitting with his head in his hands, and Bartley glanced down at him pityingly before he continued to the rest of us, "From the first, I suspected that whoever had killed Slyke had some knowledge of medicine. The average layman would not have known how to place the revolver in Slyke's hand in such a way that it would appear to be suicide. The point that puzzled me was that the eyes were almost closed. If the guilty person knew enough to place the revolver in Slyke's hand before it stiffened, he should have known that the eyes ought to be open. Miss Potter explained this discrepancy by saying that she had closed the eyes herself, frightened by their stare. Then I was baffled. True, there were the circles on the magazine, but I did not know who made them and there seemed no way of finding out. Then one day, while I was in the doctor's office, he kept drawing little figures on a pad before him as he talked. When he was called to the 'phone, I took out the piece of paper on which he had been drawing and had carelessly thrown it into a wastepaper basket as he passed. On it were the same figures that I had found on the magazine cover. Even then I was slow to believe he could be the murderer, though science had proved that a person always draws the same design. But when Briffeur's death came, I knew. I found the same symbols on the knife handle. There was but one way he could have been killed."

"My God, how?" Roche gasped out.

"The knife blow came from the front. You who sat next to the chauffeur heard nothing. No one could have crept up on him without making some sound. Therefore the knife had to be thrown."

"Thrown?" we gasped.

"Yes. That was the only way it could have reached him. The blow came from directly in front of Briffeur. It could only be thrown. Upon the knife handle were the circles such as I had found elsewhere. Someone had scratched them on it in a moment of idleness. It was a trench knife. Doctor King had been to the front; he was the only one directly in front of Briffeur, .and the only one who could have thrown it. We had all agreed that Briffeur was killed because he knew who had murdered Slyke, and that the same man murdered them both. There is another proof, also. The only person, outside of the family, that the dog liked was Doctor King. The day we found Slyke dead the dog came in, growled at the rest of us but let King pat him."

The doctor raised his head, his face white save for two red spots in either cheek. His eyes were pools of blazing light. He looked at us wildly for a second, then threw out his hands and in a voice, low at first but growing louder as he continued, he admitted, "Yes, I killed them. I never intended to do so, God knows! It all goes back some time."

Bartley interrupted him. "To the time when you got mixed up with Slyke and Briffeur, selling whiskey?"

"Yes—yes, that was it. It goes back to that." His voice faltered, then he recovered. 'I came back from the war, broke. Slyke suggested that I go in with him on running whiskey. I had a camp and fast motor boat on Lake Champlain; it was all I did have. He suggested we run the whiskey down the lake from Canada to my camp, then bring it on here and hide it in the vault. He never played fair with us; he cheated us again and again. That's why Briffeur suggested we break into the house and see if he had told the truth about the amount of money he said he got for it. He kept the records of all our sales in his safe. We tried to—you know the rest about the robbery."

His voice trailed off into a whisper. I recalled that he had been shell shocked, and wondered if he could stand the strain he was undergoing.

"The night I was at Currie's to dinner and met Mr. Bartley it was Slyke who called me up on the 'phone."

His voice was shrill now, and I thought he would break down at any moment.

"He said he wished to see me, and I started over here. I ran into Briffeur, who told me that Slyke had sold the rest of the whiskey for $23,000. Well—where was I?" He stopped, confused, and passed his hand over his face.

"Oh, yes—the whiskey. I went up to the tower, and he suggested we go out on the balcony,—why, I don't know. I asked him what he got for the whiskey, and he said $10,000. I knew he lied, and I told him so. We quarreled, quarreled. All at once, he flashed a revolver on me and said he had a good mind to kill me—he had been drinking."

Again his voice trailed away into silence and his eyes closed. Then he recovered himself with an effort and continued, "Just what happened then, I don't know— don't know! My nerves have been in pieces since I was shell shocked. We struggled, and I know I shot him. I did as you say. Took him downstairs, undressed him, and put the revolver in his hand. I knew—knew—that most people would think he had killed himself. I was desperately sorry —but I am hardly to blame for his death. My big mistake was calling in Mr. Bartley the next morning. I knew, if I could fool him, I could fool everyone."

He paused; his head sank again into his hands. I saw that Bartley pitied him deeply and his voice was soft and his face grave as he asked, "And Briffeur?"

With an effort the doctor raised his head.

"I was always afraid of that man. He was cruel and treacherous. When I saw him at the inquest I knew that

all was over; that he would give me away. And when the
lights went out, in a wild rage I threw that knife. I don't
know why." Then he almost yelled, "I wanted peace."

"But how did you happen to have the knife with you?"
Bartley asked.

He thought for a moment. It seemed hard for him to
gather himself together enough to answer, "I don't
know—oh, yes, I had used it to cut a strap on my car.
When I arrived here the day of the inquest, I found I had
left it on the floor and I put it in my bag. There was a bag
on the table all the time, you remember. "

It was easy to see that the doctor was in such a
nervous collapse that he could say no more; he slumped
down in his chair and closed his eyes. There was some
whispered conversation between Roche and Bartley; and
then, as if not liking the task, Roche went over and placed
his hand on the doctor's shoulder. At his touch the doctor
stiffened. He knew too well what it meant. Shaking off
the hand, he slowly rose and walked, with an effort, to
where Bartley stood.

"Mr. Bartley," he said, his voice trembling, "will you
shake hands with me? I bear you no ill will. It's a long
journey before me."

Into Bartley's eyes came a look of comprehending pity,
and even admiration. He grasped his hand and silently
the two men, one a murderer, the other the detective that
had apprehended him, looked into each other's eyes. Then
slowly their hands fell apart and Roche led Doctor King
from the room.

None of us spoke until Bartley broke the silence by
saying, almost in a whisper, "Poor chap! God alone knows
what he has gone through."

After a little he added, "There was more I could have
said. The evidence against the doctor was made up of
various little things, all of them conclusive. There were
the cigarettes found in the tower room. They were of the
same brand King smoked. Then there was a little stopper
from a bottle that had held some kind of vaccine. Only a

doctor would have that about him. How he chanced to lose it I don't know. All this evidence, however, is too slight to have convicted him before any jury in the world. He had only to keep still and say nothing, and he was safe. He has not been a well man since his return from the war, and my only way of proving him a murderer was that a sudden shock might make him speak. I wish I had not had to do it that way. Then there is another thing! The chauffeur, you remember, pointed ahead of him as he died, saying, "I—killed." If he had been in the same position in which he was when the knife struck him, he would have been pointing directly at Doctor King. All this evidence is so slight that, if he had only kept still, he would have been safe.

"The butler told me," he concluded, "that while we were up on the balcony Doctor King returned to the room for his hat. This gave him the chance to remove the gun from Slyke's hand. No one else had the opportunity."

Suddenly Currie demanded, "John, what about those slates and that awful ghost? I never was so scared in my life."

For the first time a smile crossed Bartley's face.

"The slates? Why I wrote the messages."

"You! But we washed them," Currie exclaimed.

"Surely, you washed them. That was the whole trick. I wrote those messages with a camel's hair brush in hydrochloric acid with a bit of zinc in it. When that mixture is washed with water, the writing is blotted out until the slate dries again. You remember I always washed one side first; that was the side with the writing on it. Then I let you wash the other; and, of course, that made you sure that there was nothing on the slate. Had you not seen it washed with your own eyes? When the slate dried, the writing simply reappeared."

Miss Potter had been sitting, overcome by what had taken place. But as Bartley's explanation ceased she cried, "Then I did not receive a message from Mr. Slyke?"

"No, Miss Potter," Bartley said apologetically, "you did not. You must forgive me. I knew that King was guilty, and I had to make him confess by frightening or startling him into saying something that could be used against him. He half believed in spiritualism, and I thought that if I could stage a séance I might make him confess. There was a medium in New York I had once saved from jail and I brought him here with two assistants."

"But the raps?" she questioned.

"Oh, I produced the raps. Almost all of that sort of thing is a fake, you know. You remember that I had you place your hands on the table. Then I rose and turned out the lights. When I came back I slipped you the thumb and little finger of my right hand. You thought, of course, that both my hands were being held. They were not. You only held one, while the other was free to give the raps. The medium was tied and gagged, but you can't tie one of those chaps so securely that they cannot speak and move when they want to."

Currie gave a long sigh of disappointment. "Then I never saw a ghost at all?"

"No, Bob," came the answer, "you did not. Everything was staged to lead up to the words you heard that figure say. What you saw was one of the medium's assistants painted with phosphorus so that he would glow in the dark. He was covered with a black velvet bag, made in sections; and another man, wearing black gloves and a mask to make him invisible, removed the sections of the bag one by one. This gave him the appearance of materializing suddenly out of the air. The head was a mask modeled from a photograph of Slyke. When the figure vanished, the second man had simply covered him from head to foot with a black cloth, thus blotting him from your sight. The whole trick has been used again and again by so called mediums."

Currie looked at his friend admiringly. "I must confess, John," he said, "you gave me a bad half hour. I was scared stiff."

We laughed sympathetically, for we had each experienced the same fear.

Black rose to his feet saying, "Mr. Bartley, you have solved three problems by one solution—the two murders and the robbery."

As Bartley was about to answer the telephone rang and he left the room as if he had anticipated the message. We could hear his cool, low voice say, "Yes, this is Mr. Bartley. Yes, Roche. No—I am not surprised. It's the best thing, after all, that could have happened."

When he returned to us his face was very grave and sad, yet with something of relief in it.

"Roche tells me," he said slowly, "that when he reached the station King was dead. Suicide."

The news did not startle me. I, too, felt relieved. Bartley was silent a moment, playing with the bag before him on the table. Suddenly he raised his head.

"You know he wished to say good by to me. I knew then what he was going to do. I could have had him searched and have prevented it, but it is better so. He has not been himself for months; we will never know all that he has suffered. I am sorry for him. What a great darkness must have covered his life for the last few days! Now it is over."

He was silent again for a moment, and then added, "He took the best way out of the affair."

THE END

Other Resurrected Press Books in *The Chief Inspector Pointer Mystery* Series

Murder at Bridge

When an afternoon bridge party attended by some of Hamilton's leading citizens ends with the hostess being murdered in her boudoir, Special Investigator Dundee of the District Attorney's office is called in. But one of the attendees is guilty? There are plenty of suspects: the victim's former lover, her current suitor, the retired judge who is being blackmailed, the victim's maid who had been horribly disfigured accidentally by the murdered woman, or any of the women who's husbands had flirted with the victim. Or was she murdered by an outsider whose motive had nothing to do with the town of Hamilton. Find the answer in... **Murder at Bridge**

One Drop of Blood

When Dr. Koenig, head of Mayfield Sanitarium is murdered, the District Attorney's Special Investigator, "Bonnie" Dundee must go undercover to find the killer. Were any of the inmates of the asylum insane enough to have committed the crime? Or, was it one of the staff, motivated by jealousy? And what was is the secret in the murdered man's past. Find the answer in... **One Drop of Blood**

AVAILABLE FROM RESURRECTED PRESS!

THE EDWARDIAN DETECTIVES
LITERARY SLEUTHS OF THE EDWARDIAN ERA

The exploits of the great Victorian Detectives, Poe's C. Auguste Dupin, Gaboriau's Lecoq, and most famously, Arthur Conan Doyle's Sherlock Holmes, are well known. But what of those fictional detectives that came after, those of the Edwardian Age? The period between the death of Queen Victoria and the First World War had been called the Golden Age of the detective short story, but how familiar is the modern reader with the sleuths of this era? And such an extraordinary group they were, including in their numbers an unassuming English priest, a blind man, a master of disguises, a lecturer in medical jurisprudence, a noble woman working for Scotland Yard, and a savant so brilliant he was known as "The Thinking Machine."

To introduce readers to these detectives, Resurrected Press has assembled a collection of stories featuring these and other remarkable sleuths in The Edwardian Detectives.

- The Case of Laker, Absconded by Arthur Morrison
- The Fenchurch Street Mystery by Baroness Orczy
- The Crime of the French Café by Nick Carter
- The Man with Nailed Shoes by R Austin Freeman
- The Blue Cross by G. K. Chesterton
- The Case of the Pocket Diary Found in the Snow by Augusta Groner
- The Ninescore Mystery by Baroness Orczy
- The Riddle of the Ninth Finger by Thomas W. Hanshew
- The Knight's Cross Signal Problem by Ernest Bramah

- The Problem of Cell 13 by Jacques Futrelle
- The Conundrum of the Golf Links by Percy James Brebner
- The Silkworms of Florence by Clifford Ashdown
- The Gateway of the Monster by William Hope Hodgson
- The Affair at the Semiramis Hotel by A. E. W. Mason
- The Affair of the Avalanche Bicycle & Tyre Co., LTD by Arthur Morrison

RESURRECTED PRESS CLASSIC MYSTERY CATALOGUE

Journeys into Mystery
Travel and Mystery in a More Elegant Time

The Edwardian Detectives
Literary Sleuths of the Edwardian Era

Gems of Mystery
Lost Jewels from a More Elegant Age

E. C. Bentley
Trent's Last Case: The Woman in Black

Ernest Bramah
Max Carrados Resurrected:
The Detective Stories of Max Carrados

Agatha Christie
The Secret Adversary
The Mysterious Affair at Styles

Octavus Roy Cohen
Midnight

Freeman Wills Croft
The Ponson Case
The Pit Prop Syndicate

J. S. Fletcher
The Herapath Property
The Rayner-Slade Amalgamation
The Chestermarke Instinct
The Paradise Mystery
Dead Men's Money

The Middle of Things
Ravensdene Court
Scarhaven Keep
The Orange-Yellow Diamond
The Middle Temple Murder
The Tallyrand Maxim
The Borough Treasurer
In the Mayor's Parlour
The Saftey Pin

R. Austin Freeman

The Mystery of 31 New Inn from the Dr. Thorndyke Series
John Thorndyke's Cases from the Dr. Thorndyke Series
The Red Thumb Mark from The Dr. Thorndyke Series
The Eye of Osiris from The Dr. Thorndyke Series
A Silent Witness from the Dr. John Thorndyke Series
The Cat's Eye from the Dr. John Thorndyke Series
Helen Vardon's Confession: A Dr. John Thorndyke Story
As a Thief in the Night: A Dr. John Thorndyke Story
Mr. Pottermack's Oversight: A Dr. John Thorndyke Story
Dr. Thorndyke Intervenes: A Dr. John Thorndyke Story
The Singing Bone: The Adventures of Dr. Thorndyke
The Stoneware Monkey: A Dr. John Thorndyke Story
The Great Portrait Mystery, and Other Stories: A Collection of Dr. John Thorndyke and Other Stories
The Penrose Mystery: A Dr. John Thorndyke Story
The Uttermost Farthing: A Savant's Vendetta

Arthur Griffiths

The Passenger From Calais
The Rome Express

Fergus Hume
The Mystery of a Hansom Cab
The Green Mummy
The Silent House
The Secret Passage

Edgar Jepson
The Loudwater Mystery

A. E. W. Mason
At the Villa Rose

A. A. Milne
The Red House Mystery
Baroness Emma Orczy
The Old Man in the Corner

Edgar Allan Poe
The Detective Stories of Edgar Allan Poe

Arthur J. Rees
The Hampstead Mystery
The Shrieking Pit
The Hand In The Dark
The Moon Rock
The Mystery of the Downs

Mary Roberts Rinehart
Sight Unseen and The Confession

Dorothy L. Sayers
Whose Body?

Sir William Magnay
The Hunt Ball Mystery

Mabel and Paul Thorne
The Sheridan Road Mystery

Louis Tracy
The Strange Case of Mortimer Fenley
The Albert Gate Mystery
The Bartlett Mystery
The Postmaster's Daughter
The House of Peril
The Sandling Case: What Would You Have Done?
Charles Edmonds Walk
The Paternoster Ruby

John R. Watson
The Mystery of the Downs
The Hampstead Mystery

Edgar Wallace
The Daffodil Mystery
The Crimson Circle

Carolyn Wells
Vicky Van
The Man Who Fell Through the Earth
In the Onyx Lobby
Raspberry Jam
The Clue
The Room with the Tassels
The Vanishing of Betty Varian
The Mystery Girl
The White Alley
The Curved Blades
Anybody but Anne
The Bride of a Moment
Faulkner's Folly
The Diamond Pin
The Gold Bag
The Mystery of the Sycamore
The Come Backy

Raoul Whitfield
Death in a Bowl

And much more!
Visit ResurrectedPress.com
for our complete catalogue

About Resurrected Press

A division of Intrepid Ink, LLC, Resurrected Press is dedicated to bringing high quality, vintage books back into publication. See our entire catalogue and find out more at www.ResurrectedPress.com.

About Intrepid Ink, LLC

Intrepid Ink, LLC provides full publishing services to authors of fiction and non-fiction books, eBooks and websites. From editing to formatting, from publishing to marketing, Intrepid Ink gets your creative works into the hands of the people who want to read them. Find out more at www.IntrepidInk.com.

www.ingramcontent.com/pod-product-compliance
Lightning Source LLC
Chambersburg PA
CBHW070003260626
47159CB00005B/1651